WHITE HORSE POINT

What Reviewers Say
About Andrews & Austin's Work

Combust the Sun

"In a succinct film-style narrative, with scenes that move, a character-driven plot, and crisp dialogue worthy of a screenplay, Andrews & Austin have successfully crafted an engaging Hollywood mystery."—*Midwest Book Review*

Summer Winds

"Andrews & Austin never, never disappoint their fans. Their wit and intelligence sing from the pages."—*Just About Write*

Uncross My Heart

"The one-liners come fast and furiously, but it's the relationship between two bright, intelligent women that resonates long after the last page has been turned."—Ellen Hart, Lambda Literary Award-winning author of the Jane Lawless Mystery series.

"Andrews & Austin weave religion and romance together in a story that tackles a serious issue with bracing humor, and that balances provocative thought with sensual entertainment."—Richard Labonte, *Q-Syndicate*

Mistress of the Runes

"With its humorous depiction of glamorous careers and corporate shenanigans, in *Mistress of the Runes*, Andrews & Austin once again offer readers sheer entertainment. They manage to playfully sustain a teasing erotic tension from beginning to end, but the heart of the book is its dollop of Sarah-Dreher-style mysticism. It is also somewhat reminiscent of Virginia Woolf's *Orlando*: 'Warrior queen, working on love and fear while wearing different costumes…fear gets love out of balance, doesn't it?'"
—Lee Lynch, author of *Sweet Creek*

"On the surface, this novel is about finding one's way back from repeated failed romances, but Brice Chandler's struggles encompass so much more. This sometimes serious, sometimes funny and always touching story can teach us all a lesson about living our dreams and following fate, whether we believe in it or not."—*Story Circle Book Reviews*

"Andrews and Austin have backgrounds in the entertainment and news industries, and I enjoyed the insight into worlds far removed from my own. Their combined knowledge and talent are demonstrated in the composition of *Mistress of the Runes*. This book does not move quickly or rashly, but with a combination of dry humor, believable dialogue (both internal and spoken), and a touch of the paranormal, Brice Chandler's story will stay with the reader."—*Midwest Book Review*

Stellium in Scorpio

"Appealing lead characters that possess wit and intelligence drive this novel. Richfield and Rivers make a wonderful couple

who experience the various ups and downs of life with a sense of humor, affection, patience…and an astrology chart."
—*L-word.com Literature*

"Appealing lead characters that possess wit and intelligence drive this novel. The dialogue is smart, humorous, and realistically expressed."—*Just About Write*

Venus Besieged

"*Venus Besieged* skillfully weaves the beliefs of Native Americans with astrology, creating an exciting read."—*Just About Write*

Visit us at www.boldstrokesbooks.com

By the Authors

Combust The Sun

Stellium In Scorpio

Mistress of the Runes

Venus Besieged

Uncross My Heart

Summer Winds

White Horse Point

WHITE HORSE POINT

by

Andrews & Austin

2020

WHITE HORSE POINT

ISBN 13: 978-1-63555-695-7

This Trade Paperback Original Is Published By
Bold Strokes Books, Inc.
P.O. Box 249
Valley Falls, NY 12185

First Edition: April 2020

CREDITS
Editor: Shelley Thrasher
Production Design: Susan Ramundo
Cover Design By Tammy Seidick

Acknowledgments

Our heartfelt thanks to Radclyffe and BSB for supporting our work, and to our wonderful editor, Dr. Shelley Thrasher, for her input and guidance. Thank you to Connie Ward, our friend who has played many roles at BSB over the years. We appreciate the hard work of the BSB team, led by Sandy Lowe. Special thanks to Laurie Hedlund of Hedlund Dressage for equine technical assistance. And we thank all of our readers who for a decade have encouraged us to once again write lesbian fiction.

Dedication

To Rachel Maddow for her intelligence, tenacity,
and bravery in covering the important news
when no one else is paying attention.

CHAPTER ONE

I feel like I'm just waiting. Waiting to live, waiting to die, waiting for the other shoe to drop, trying to figure out what to do while I wait, and wondering if whatever I'm waiting for will even be worth it." I ran my hand through my hair and leaned back in the cushy club chair at the Algonquin, famous for its literary history and the lights in the Blue Bar, where after two martinis, you couldn't tell your agent from an alien.

I crossed my leg, revealing an Italian-weave loafer, and slid my fingers nervously down the pleat of my Armani slacks. The matching tan vest seemed tight, so I opened the bottom button, then loosened my tie, and finally stopped fidgeting. I'd made a fashion effort only because Ramona, one of New York's more fabled publicists, liked her lunch guests to be "well put together."

"When I write…" I said.

"Used to write." Ramona corrected me and nonchalantly scanned the room for people she might know.

"Unkind," I said evenly.

"You have mid-life angst." She delivered her Holiday Inn diagnosis with only minor compassion, while making a failed attempt at surreptitiously checking her watch. "You're just in one of your dark periods."

Ramona was a true New Yorker—perfectly coiffed silver hair, seventy but sexy, black suit, gym-trim body, big diamonds, and short attention span.

"Stop being depressed," she said.

"How can I *not* be depressed? Everyone in New York wears black. I feel like I'm in *Game of Thrones*."

Ramona texted while absently addressing me and never making eye contact. "Taylor, I want you to take the rest of the summer and go up North to the lake."

"The mosquitos are large enough to be wall art," I said, as Ramona dipped into her tiny purse with two fingers. "Why do you bother with a four-inch purse? Don't you have a pocket?"

"This purse cost a thousand dollars per square inch, and every woman in here appreciates that fact but you." She extracted an old, rust-colored skeleton key and slid it across the cocktail table's high-gloss surface.

I pushed it back and flung the back of my hand to my forehead, imitating someone about to be exiled. "Nooo. Anything but the key!"

Ramona pushed the key forward again. "Your aunt Alice knew what she was doing when she built that cabin, and even more when she sold it to me. Take the key and think about it. Better yet, just go to the cabin, breathe, and finish the damned book!"

I hugged her, thanked her for the lunch, tucked the key into my vest pocket, and left the Algonquin, melding into the flood of people hurrying along West Forty-fourth. I could send the key back to her with a nice note. I didn't have to travel to hell and gone to write.

Two blocks farther, I stopped at Kaddish's Deli to pick something up for dinner, where I stood in line waiting to order alongside a throng of irritable people crowding the meat case. The muscular man behind the counter in a sweat-stained T-shirt shouted in a Bronx accent, "In line over there!" He caught sight of me. "Hey, honey, what?"

"I'll have the chicken salad sandwich." As he scooped it up, two flies landed on the open tray of chicken salad. "Never mind. Keep the insect sandwich. I'll have the mac and cheese."

"Listen at you! Keep the insect sandwich! That's free protein!" He was still joking with me as I grabbed the mac and cheese, plus a green salad, in a plastic box and paid the cashier. "Her Royal Highness don't want flies on her chicken salad. She's got no idea what's in the mac and cheese!" He was right about that.

A block away, I tried to hail a cab as three of them zipped past me, their lights off, indicating they had a passenger or perhaps were just ignoring me. Looking back toward Forty-second, I saw two other people trying to flag a cab head of me. All of us, two feet off the sidewalk waving our arms frantically like human windmills.

If I weren't insane, I would go crazy, I thought, and ducked into the subway, no longer trusting Uber drivers not to kill me. And to think some people were willing to text Turo and hook up with a total stranger and rent their personal car. And what if when they picked up the car, the guy killed them, or had a stash of drugs hidden inside the door, and the cops pulled them over, or the guy was a gang leader and a rival gang had been waiting for his car— the one they just rented—to drive by, and boom, they were dead! I'm good at thinking things through to their morbid conclusion, which is probably why I write...used to write...mysteries.

The hot, sweaty, body-odor-cum-food stench of summer underground told me I'd made a bad decision. Turo no longer sounded terrible.

Twenty feet to my right, a man oddly dressed for the intense heat of summer, in sweats and a hoodie, stood beside a woman wearing a fast-food uniform and a scarf tied under her chin. Suddenly he shouted something and pushed her in front of the oncoming train.

My heart slapped against my chest, and my knees momentarily collapsed. Two burly, middle-aged men shouted at him and instantly set chase, as the crowd screamed.

A skinny black man, in dirty jeans and torn tennis shoes, leapt over the side of the cement platform, his dreadlocks swinging around his head like ropes at a rodeo, and yanked the woman off the rails literally seconds before the train blew by. The crowd-squeals increased two octaves.

Several people helped pull her back up to safety. She was battered from the fall, with a gash on her forehead where blood streamed down onto her face and dripped onto her burger uniform. A man ripped off his shirt and tied it like a tourniquet around her head, and the bleeding slowed, and we could see she hadn't lost her arms or legs or her life. Then other men in the crowd hoisted her rescuer back up, as everyone cheered and clapped for the man who looked like he had nothing to lose if the train had killed him too.

"You're a hero!" someone shouted, and several people reached out to touch him, the way gamblers do when someone wins and they want the good fortune to rub off on them.

"Thanks, man," he said with a half-smile and wandered off.

Transit security raced down the platform, and a medic came forward out of the crowd and knelt beside the injured woman. The two burly men had the pusher pinned to the ground when police arrived and cuffed him. The rest of us squawked our disbelief at one another like terrified geese.

"I can't fucking believe that!" I shouted into the air, and people echoed me.

"Fucking crazy bastard!"

"Holy shit!"

There was nothing more for any of us to do but continue to quiver and move on. I tried to climb back up the subway stairs to get some air, my legs as useless as broken bow strings. I could hear the authorities in the background questioning the poor woman, and her weak, trembling reply. "I don't know. I was just waiting for the train."

I forced my shaky legs to propel me down the sidewalk to a brick high-rise on Sixty-eighth Street. I took the elevator, still clutching my deli dinner, and got off on the eleventh floor, then realized the door to my apartment was unlocked. The super was inside trying to get my air-conditioning to work.

"I was just in the subway, and a guy pushed a woman in front of the train!" I squeaked, grateful to have someone to tell.

"No kidding?" He grabbed the back of his pants and gave them a hoist, relocating the tool belt on his tall, lanky frame. Then he glanced over his shoulder at me for a second before tinkering with the AC again. "People are nuts!" He ran his large hand through his dark, curly hair.

That was the extent of it—so much drama in the city that nothing, not even my first-hand account of a woman being pushed in front of a subway train, could rise above the level of "people are nuts."

I stashed my salad in the fridge, alongside the mac and cheese, and waited for the super to generate cool air.

"Can't fix it," he finally announced. "You'll have to wait till Thursday, when the AC people can get to it."

"It's almost August. I've suffered long enough! I could die of heat stroke by Thursday. You've got to fix it."

"Would if I could." I glowered at him, and he shrugged. "Hey, what do you want from me?"

"Who are you, Adam Lambert?" I asked as the door clicked shut behind him.

I looked around the apartment at the tall bookshelves that required a ladder for dusting, the tiny kitchen with its old-fashioned fridge, the windows in need of washing that ran the length of the living room, where the old radiator provided heat in winter. Ironically the only thing missing was cool air in summer, and it was fucking summer!

I'd chosen not to sink my divorce funds into a more expensive apartment, so I'd settled for kitschy. And as I thought about that, I was suddenly angry and not even sure what I was angry about. I paused to look up at the ceiling at whatever guides or gods were assigned to me and said irritably, "Something has to change!"

I yanked a green canvas duffel bag from under my wrought-iron bed. A wrought-iron bed just screamed that I was having sex with no one, because a metal headboard was simply asking for a concussion. I started packing—designer jeans, boots, tennis shoes, political-statement sweatshirts, low-rise underwear, socks, shorts, T-shirt, sweats, and a nightshirt.

Finished, I rang Ramona. "I'm going. You'll see me back here in the fall when my ass is so frozen, they'll have to ship me home in an ice chest."

Ramona seemed genuinely happy. "Good! Are you flying?"

"I hate to fly! Watch *Nightly News.* Everyone dies. The ventilation has Legionnaires' disease, the kid next to you gives you measles, and then you crash on the Max 8."

"So you're flying." Ramona spoke in a flat, disinterested tone that ignored my commentary and indicated she had something more critical going on.

"I'm wearing red so they'll spot me in the wreckage and rescue me first."

Ramona focused in. "Taylor, from angst comes great writing. But when you reach black-hole depression, no one wants to read what you have to say. You need a little joy in your life. Fly out to Minnesota tomorrow. I'll call Marney and tell her you're coming, and to get things ready for you."

"How do you have an intimate relationship with a neighbor a thousand miles away when I don't even know who lives next door to me?" I asked her, while holding my phone to my ear with my shoulder and evaluating whether I should pack one nice sweater and a pair of slacks.

"I'm a publicist. We're intimate with everyone," Ramona said. "Get a hot-stone massage and a facial before you go. You're a great-looking woman, but who would know."

"Thanks. I'm sure the bears will appreciate me arriving all tenderized."

"With your height, those shoulders, and that short platinum hair, it takes a very confident man to approach you, Cersei," she teased, picking up on my *Game of Thrones* reference and labeling me the difficult queen. "Fluff it up a little! And for God's sake, lose the tie. You might meet someone. Imagine that! It's been years since Ben, and you were at least writing during all that drama."

"Maybe I'll meet a homicidal lumberjack who tries to chop me up for cord wood, and you can be happy again. Can I get internet up there?"

"It's not the moon, Taylor. Yes, DSL. But if phone lines are down, then internet is down."

"I love it when you talk tech." I teased her. "I'll call when I get there."

Ramona was right. After Ben, I couldn't write. I was pissed at myself for ever having been with him in the first place and putting up with his needling comments about me. Though I'd told myself I could ignore what he said, it had gotten into my psyche and made me numb. I couldn't write numb.

Income from the divorce was the one benefit of my having been married. We split everything down the middle because he didn't want an argument—that was after we'd argued for three months. He didn't want anyone to know why I was divorcing him—abusive wasn't the descriptor he wanted to be tagged with. He had that perfect, beneficent, kind-hearted image to preserve for his coworkers and friends. God only knew what he said about me after I left, but it couldn't have been much worse than what he said to me while we were together.

I looked in the full-length mirror. I was five foot eight, and my blond hair was intentionally Emma Thompson—short on the sides, with the high swoosh falling over my right eye.

I'm tall and big boned. How would that particular combination age? *Not well. Ask a dinosaur.*

My green eyes were fired up and jumped out at me, probably because my skin was pale and in need of something…ah, yes, facial cream. I opened a jar at random and applied the thick, white formula. My cheekbones were prominent and my jawline strong, but my smile was my most winning attribute. Men always came across the room to chat—if I smiled at them—which of late I tried not to do.

I examined the other jars stacked on my cramped bathroom counter, each touting a different benefit—lifts and holds, moisturizes and rejuvenates, erases lines and dark spots. Then why did women over sixty look like exhausted leopards? *Relax. You're not there yet. You're a youthful forty-seven.*

"I think I need rejuvenating," I said out loud, and tossed that particular jar into my cosmetic kit. *Maybe I'll lie on the dock and get a tan. Or maybe not.* I checked my figure in the full-length mirror. It actually wasn't bad. However, I did long for bathing suits that covered me from wrist to ankle; they were charming. I didn't even own a bathing suit. I was firm but not buffed. Everyone in the damned city was toned, or muscled, and working out in the rooftop spa at four thirty a.m. *What's the point of exercising if, when you quit for a week, you go back to what you were? I'm strong but soft.* I was trying to make myself feel better. Based on the men I'd known, the confident ones, as Ramona would say, soft did seem to draw a crowd. *Screw it. I'll buy a bathing suit up there if I decide to go in the lake.*

I was up at dawn, put on a pair of trim gray slacks, a tailored white shirt tucked in with a gray designer belt, and gray mesh loafers, then grabbed a cab and headed for LaGuardia. In line at the airport, the older, well-coiffed man ahead of me was giving his wife the third degree about what she'd packed for him. He was dressed in logo-festooned golf attire, minus the cleats. His head was on a swivel, scouting the terminal and pausing when he saw a pretty girl while continuing the conversation with his wife. "I told you not to forget that. How hard is that to remember?" He reminded me of Ben—nice looking, but not nice. *She should tell him to stick his putter up his ass.*

Ben could be funny, I mused, which is what attracted me to him, but I didn't love him. And once we stopped partying and sobered up, it became apparent he was very bad in bed. We stopped having sex almost immediately. I wanted something more but made no attempt to get it, a fact I'd re-examined incessantly over the last four years. Was I in a trance, under his spell, lazy and not giving a damn, or what? I just hung in and put up with it.

What irony! The times when things were "okay" in our relationship seemed to be a reason to put up with the times that were horrible. Okay wasn't supposed to be the condition of marriage. Okay was your condition in the ER: "He's lost his left leg, but he's going to be okay."

I had two lives—the self-assured author doing interviews and book signings; and the wife, in name only, who'd stopped focusing on what she wanted and just learned to want less. My decade with Ben had been a total waste of time...pointless! *Wind yourself up, tear yourself down. Let up!*

I didn't realize I was glowering at the man in front of me, who shot me a "what's up with you, lady?" look. I quickly changed my expression, almost smiling at him, then caught myself in time to keep from acquiescing. *I should be able to glower if I want to.*

After an hour of waiting, we trekked down the jetway and boarded. I pushed my duffel into the overhead bin above my seat and buckled myself in, my heart rate increasing dramatically, my fear level rising. It didn't matter if the weather was perfection, or if the pilot was Sully Sullenberger, or if John the Baptist materialized to assure me I'd have an equal number of takeoffs and landings. I didn't want to be trapped in a silver tube 30,000 feet above the ground with no control over what might happen. Flying meant I trusted that the guy who tightened the screws on the engine wasn't on meth, and the guy who loaded the cargo wasn't an Al Qaeda sympathizer. I didn't trust. I didn't want to feel that way, but I did.

A dark-haired woman in her early fifties sat down next to me in the aisle seat. She was wearing jodhpurs and shiny paddock boots, looking like something out of a European riding journal.

Strange attire for a plane flight. Where was she going that required she arrive ready to ride?

"Angelique," she introduced herself, and I thought I knew her from somewhere—maybe a literary conference.

"Taylor James," I said.

"You look rather dashing." Her eyes danced over me.

"I was going to say the same of you." I smiled.

"But you didn't."

"Synaptic delay," I said, amused that she seemed to speak unedited.

"Going to the Northwoods?" Her voice was silky.

"I guess so."

"You don't sound very excited about it."

"I don't seem to get excited much lately. Actually, I do get excited, just not happily excited." I smiled at her again. She was lovely.

"You have important work to do there."

"That's what my publicist says," and I laughed. "But I've lost the passion."

"You can't lose what you never had," she said.

How presumptuous! Why the hell do people think they have the right to analyze me? I was about to cut the conversation short when she gave a cosmic shrug. "Well, the Northwoods will change all that."

"All what?"

"Your passion. You'll find passion you never knew existed."

"How do you know that?"

"I've been there." She patted me on the knee in a familiar fashion and gave me a wicked grin. "Allow me to be excited on your behalf."

The stewardess interrupted to ask me what I'd like to drink as the woman slid out of her seat and headed for the bathroom. She was tall and glamorous and a bit 1970s. "This is going to be a very nice flight," she said absently over her shoulder.

She didn't return, and another passenger took her seat. I told the stewardess that I thought a woman, the one in jodhpurs, was sitting there. The stewardess seemed perplexed, saying she hadn't seen anyone. I walked the aisle front to back before we were told to take our seats and fasten our seatbelts. I didn't see anyone either.

Well, that's the damndest thing, I said to myself, then fell into a deep sleep.

I was surprised when the sound of the wheels touching down woke me up. I never slept on a plane. Never.

CHAPTER TWO

Minneapolis was the city I always thought New York would be if she were an over-sexed teenager—energetic, beautiful, and accepting, with great orchestras, wonderful art, think-tank universities, high-minded politics, and liberal leanings. Aunt Alice always said she liked Minnesotans because they didn't meddle in your bedroom, your politics, or your mental state, but you paid the price in winters so brutal they'd remove your first three layers of skin.

A Chevy SUV was the rental company's only four-wheel-drive vehicle, so I took it, eager to start my five-hour drive due north. Living in the land of Lyfts and limos, I hadn't driven in a while, so it was liberating to be behind the wheel.

The roads were winding and well cared for, lined with gargantuan pine trees that let the flickering sunlight splatter intermittently onto the forest floor. Beaver dams protruded above the surface of big clear ponds, and the state lived up to its slogan, "Land of 10,000 Lakes"—big lakes, small lakes, clean and crystal-clear lakes that came right up to the edge of the road and threatened to spill over. Little tackle shops and beer joints sprang up—their tiny gravel parking spots the only dry space between the beer bars and the whitecaps.

Driving closer and closer to the Canadian border, I was in awe of the sheer size of nearly everything and unnerved by how close the lakes were to the road. I wanted to reach my destination before dark to avoid driving into one.

Finally I spotted the sign up ahead proclaiming MUSKIE MINNESOTA, THE MUSKIE CAPITAL OF THE WORLD, POPULATION 989. I drove through town, past the drugstore and coffee shop on one side and the trading post and hardware store on the other, and parked in front of Muskie Market to gather a few groceries.

The moment I entered the store, the woman behind the grocery counter looked me over with a wide grin. "Alice Armand's niece, right? Marney said you were comin'. Said you haven't been here since you were a little kid, back before your aunt died." I said that was true. "I'm Helen Thorston. We own the store."

She was a big, strong, sensible-looking woman. Sensible being code for no makeup. She extended a hand connected to an arm as large as an oak limb. My hand disappeared in hers as we shook. *She has to be gay.* Not a politically correct thought, but truthfully, how many straight women did I know who could crush my hand like a walnut?

Then Thor Thorston came around the corner in his grocer's apron, blood-stained and looking like he'd either been cutting beef or leading a Viking raid.

He was a foot taller than Helen and a foot wider, with unruly red curls and a dense red beard. His overly large white teeth protruded from beneath his bushy red mustache whenever he spoke. By his side, Helen no longer looked like she might be gay, but more like the two of them might be Nordic giants…or a Nordic giant and a giant Nordic beaver.

"Hi. I'm Thor," he boomed. "You're staying in Ramona's cabin. You know that's going to be right up here on 116 and east about fifteen miles. You'll see the sign. Her cabin is number one, the reddish cabin, and the mailbox has her name on it. She's got the lights and phone working, but you get no cell-phone reception up there. You have a key, ya?" he asked in that decidedly Norwegian lilt, and I nodded. "You need something, you shout real loud," he commanded, and disappeared into the back of the store.

I grinned, contemplating that with poor phone service, I probably would have to stand in the yard and "shout real loud."

Two woven, wood-slat baskets sat beside the counter, and I picked up one and began to gather enough items to create breakfast, and maybe lunch, if I didn't mind a peanut-butter sandwich.

The store had three short rows of mostly canned items, a freezer on the north wall, a short meat case in the back, the checkout counter up front, and overhead faded tin ceiling tiles bearing images of apples and grapes, an homage to the fruits and vegetables virtually nonexistent in the store.

On the counter, I spotted a box of raspberries someone had just picked and brought in that morning, and two bananas that were so old they could have sung a few bars of "Day-O." I put them in my basket while a young redheaded boy, who looked like son-of-Thor, wrapped up a pound of hamburger for me. I laid everything on the counter for Helen to ring up.

"Staying long?" she asked.

"For the rest of the summer," I said, wondering why I'd made this spontaneous commitment to a total stranger.

"Do you know anyone out on the lake?" Helen beamed at me, seeming just happy to be alive.

"I only know I'm to meet Marney."

"Oh, for sure. She'll introduce you to everybody, you betcha," she said, rolling out the Minnesota colloquialisms, and that made me smile. Helen's enthusiasm seemed to imply that "knowing Marney" was the highest-level connection one could have in this part of the world. "Lot of tourists this time of year, so it's a good chance to meet new people."

"Everybody will be new to me," I said, and gathered up my sacked groceries. She held out a bag of peanuts. "On me. For the chipmunks. And here's a pop for the road." She handed me a Coke.

I smiled again and thanked her, thinking I was a lot more smiley than usual.

As I crawled up into the SUV, it dawned on me that not one of the businesses in town was owned by a chain or corporation, but simply by a family who ran it any way they chose. People up here seemed to feel fresh air and freedom were worth the risk of a tighter income.

❖

Driving toward the cabin, I noticed the countryside turned to narrow roads and thicker underbrush, the lakes still visible a few hundred yards off in the distance. Nonetheless I could smell the sweet, fresh water and the pine even from the road. Occasionally I'd see a curved brick dome sticking up from the ground, the top of an ancient icehouse, where elderly residents still preferred to store their ice and potatoes and meat—anything that needed to be kept cold and used throughout the summer.

In fifteen miles, I spotted a black mailbox, adjacent to three other mailboxes, on the dirt road. It was labeled #1 RYDER, Ramona's last name. I drove another two hundred yards following the barn-paint arrows that pointed visitors toward the cabin, pulled in, and parked about twenty yards from the door, which was as close as I could get. Long logs had been nailed to four tall stumps, to form two rustic hitching posts, keeping cars off the grassy lawn with its massive trees. I drew in a deep breath and felt my blood pressure drop. The view, even from the parking area, was spectacular, the lake water sparkling and dancing in the sun.

Alongside my pine-needle parking spot was an old fish-cleaning stand, where fishermen used to bring their catch straight up from the lake, clean it, and cook it all within an hour. As a child, I remembered how good the fish tasted, but nowadays I couldn't bear the idea of gasping fish being fileted. Empathy coming with age.

The cabin, made of reddish-brown logs, sat on a plateau, and the land sloped down on the far side into the lake. A boat dock stretched a hundred feet off the shore, and on the water's edge, an old red pump house probably still held fishing rods, inner tubes, and the pump that brought water up from the lake into the cabin.

The sound of the water and the wind through the pines captured me immediately. Small waves slapped against the shore, and pine needles shook in the lake breeze as I got out of the SUV and walked across the lawn, then up the back steps, and used the old skeleton key to enter. Locks up here were more polite than policing and seemed to say, "Could you give me a minute?" rather than "Keep out."

Opening the cabin door, I stepped into the tiny, old kitchen with linoleum floors, an ancient gas stove, and a battered cast-iron sink, and felt a wave of emotion. My mother and Aunt Alice used to stand here and cook and gossip when their visits overlapped. The cabin was like that—my parents would spend a week at the lake, and then they'd leave, and Aunt Alice and Uncle Jake would have the cabin to themselves for the rest of the summer. Once my parents let me stay behind, which was the only time I got to spend all summer with Aunt Alice. She was kind and funny and unafraid, and prone to locking people in the outhouse if they said something about her she didn't like. After Aunt Alice kept a man barricaded inside for four hours, installation of indoor plumbing became a priority for Uncle Jake.

One door off the kitchen led to an enclosed wraparound porch with a long row of picture windows that overlooked the lake, while a second one opened to a living room where wooden rockers, which looked like they were made of tree limbs with the bark still on them, faced the floor-to-ceiling, lake-stone fireplace.

On the kitchen wall beside the back door, Ramona had posted a laminated note that had turned brown and had smudgy fingerprints on it. Nonetheless the instructions were clear.

1) *Do not leave any food outside. It attracts raccoons and bears.*
2) *All trash goes to the dump on the back side of Hammertoe Lake, or it will attract bears.*
3) *If anything breaks, call Marney Meadows in the white cabin—phone number is by the phone. Your cell phone may not work here. You're welcome.*

There seemed to be a lot of warnings about bears.

I unloaded the groceries, then took my luggage to the large bedroom off the porch that overlooked the lake. The bed was high off the ground, soft and comfortable. On the foot of the bed, a heavy Pendleton blanket with orange, yellow, and brown stripes supported a puffy old handmade quilt with horses featured in almost every carefully sewn square. Obviously blanket choice, not thermostat, controlled the temperature.

The bed faced the lake, and the breeze through the two large bedroom windows caressed my entire body and made me think that nature still had the upper hand on happiness. If I wasn't going to have true love in this lifetime, then I at least deserved fame and fortune. And I'll love nature, I thought, stretching my arms wide and welcoming the wind into my bedroom.

I wandered back into the living room, where a modern version of an old potbellied stove gave off a gas glow. I didn't adjust the dial, being unfamiliar with any heat that wasn't piped in for a high-rise.

Inside an old writing desk, I found some 1970s postcards. One showed a picture of a local juke joint not too far from the cabin, a familiar slogan above the picture: WHEN YOU'RE OUT OF SCHLITZ, YOU'RE OUT OF BEER! The photo was faded, but I could still read the neon sign that said Jensen's. I turned it over, and someone had scrawled, "Life was complex until one day I found the point." The *L* in life had a distinctive flourish, and the stamp on the postcard had never been postmarked.

Who wrote it, and didn't send it? I wondered. And what did the writer mean by, "until one day I found the point?" I propped it up on the desk and decided to go down the road and check out Jensen's.

It was barely light outside, and I'd put in a long day, but I was inexplicably energized. It would be interesting to take in the nightlife only a mile down the lake. I put on a pair of jeans and my sneakers and a sweatshirt that said, RBG THE WOMAN FOR ME, and I headed out the door. As I drove there in only minutes, I realized it would make a nice walk along the road in the daytime.

❖

Muskie Lake was on the backside of Jensen's. I pulled onto the gravel, alongside two worn-out cars, got out feeling a bit nervous, and grabbed the aluminum door handle on the screened-in porch. Why had they bothered with a porch? The screens were floppy, and the door made a loud metallic groan as I pulled on it. Everyone in the place looked up, looked me over, and then stopped looking.

A jukebox sat directly to my left, along with three booths surrounding a pool table and floor space for dancing. Straight ahead was the bar with a door behind it that led to supplies, including tanks full of minnows and a large metal tub filled with worms. Behind the bar were beer brands known to Northerners—Bent Paddle, Snow, and Dangerous Men. Forewarned, I thought. Over the back door, a weathered board read WE PACK AND SHIP FISH.

To the right of the bar against the third wall were cabin groceries—light bulbs, ice cream, Tampax, coffee, Popsicles, cookies, marshmallows, and matches. Things you could run out of, or forget, and didn't want to drive to town to retrieve.

Three handsome, baby-stubble boys leered at me. They were blond and muscular, and I imagined earned their cut physiques the old-fashioned way, by chopping wood, rowing boats, and working in the lumber mills. The tallest one lined up a pool shot and slammed the balls with extra force, then glanced up at me and grinned. You wish, I thought.

His much shorter and cuter cohort dropped a quarter in the booth jukebox and made a few dance moves to the staticky sound system. Neon signs hung everywhere, mostly for products no longer available, like HAMM'S BEER, FROM THE LAND OF SKY-BLUE WATERS.

Jensen, a broad-chested fellow wearing suspenders, over a short-sleeved gray T-shirt, to hold up his baggy gray pants, appeared from the back of the bar, where he'd been sorting the tiny fish by size into large aerated buckets. He dried his fingers on a bar towel, gave me a big friendly grin, and asked if he could get me something. I looked at his hardworking hands, permanently dark under the nails. Worms and wieners all from the same guy, I thought, and said I was just looking.

"Take yer time," he said, and went back to sorting minnows.

I moved over to the east wall near the groceries, and that's the first time I saw her—a stunning blonde in white shorts and a white polo shirt standing at the counter carefully examining the candles for sale. The shirt was a bit plunging for a traditional polo, and it showcased her beautiful breasts.

She wasn't very tall, maybe five foot four, but she appeared tall, with her long legs and small, tight butt. *My God, her legs go to heaven.* I quickly critiqued my thoughts. *That's a male way to assess her. Wow, every guy on the lake must be after her.* However, when I glanced at the boys, none of the them were paying any attention to her.

Her profile was right out of a fashion magazine where all the faces have been air-brushed to perfection. She had the most flawless complexion. How did she maintain that out here in the woods? Not even one Muskie mosquito bite on that beautiful forehead. Her blue eyes were almost translucent and seemed otherworldly and distant, as if still focused on some faraway place she inhabited and had just momentarily left. She wore a snug ankle bracelet made of gold horses running in a circle around her beautiful leg, and the single gold band that wrapped tightly around her wrist featured two horses' heads. I wondered if she was just here on vacation, and I pretended to be looking at items near the candles as an excuse to move a little closer. Her perfume was a mixture of southern magnolias and northern pine, a diverse forest blown in off the lake. She wasn't wearing a wedding ring, I checked to see, then wondered why.

Like an exotic animal who'd been approached too quickly, she turned and disappeared through the back door. Moving casually, I left as well, trying to get a glimpse of her from the gravel drive. Maybe she was renting one of Jensen's cabins. I lost sight of her in the dark.

The blond woman had thrilled me. I could find no other word for my response. She was serendipitous. "The Lake Goddess," I dubbed her, giving me hope that interesting, sophisticated people lived nearby.

❖

Back at the cabin, I parked the car and walked the stretch to the back door, flanked by the pitch-black shadows of the pine trees, almost forgetting to be afraid of the dark.

Inside, I locked the cabin door, jumped into the big, soft bed, pulled the covers up, and was asleep almost immediately, lulled into unconsciousness by the strange sound of loons warbling to one another on the lake.

In my dream, a tall, dark-haired woman rose out of the lake and told me the wait was almost over. "It's over," she kept repeating. "It's over." I awakened in a sweat and began to fret over the parts of the dream I could remember.

How is it over? Maybe I should stay out of the lake. Maybe she's warning me I'll drown.

CHAPTER THREE

The next morning, I awoke to the sound of a lawn mower. Someone was taking care of the grass in front of the cabins. The mower's incessant buzzing in the distance was actually pleasant. I didn't hear yard maintenance in the city because there were no yards, just heat off the concrete and horns honking. By contrast, the distant hum of a mower was hypnotic, and the fresh air through my bedroom window screen was intoxicating. I felt luxuriously lazy and oddly happy.

I made a cup of coffee and then grabbed the bag of peanuts off the old Formica breakfast table, stepped outside in my nightshirt, and sat down on the wide cement steps facing the lake, enjoying the morning light.

A long dock stretched from the shore out into the sandy part of the lake, skipping the soggy clay near the bank. Shoreline clay was like glue. It sucked you down six inches into its gray muck that clung to your feet and wedged in between your toes like wet cement. You had to scrape it off before you could walk without tripping. A few feet farther out, the lake bottom became firm and then turned to amber sand that was beautiful and hard.

The view from the porch was breathtaking, and for the first time I experienced the feeling of never wanting to leave a place.

Taking a peanut from the bag, I scraped the shell on the cement and made a clicking sound with my tongue, then called chippeechippeechippee. It had been my favorite childhood activity at the cabin.

After about ten minutes, I assumed the chipmunks of my childhood were deceased, and prior to ascending to that great nuthouse in the sky, they had failed to teach their grandchildren how to panhandle for peanuts. Furthermore, sounds carried on the lake, so I was worried that Marney was listening to my ridiculous impersonation of a hungry rodent. Might as well double down on that, I thought, loudly cracking a few nuts and stuffing them into my mouth.

Suddenly peeking around the tree, a chipmunk stared at me with bright, beady eyes. I tossed a few peanuts in his direction, and he lowered his chubby little body to the ground. Soon, three chipmunks were crawling up my back and onto my shoulders, stashing the nuts in their expandable jowls and making brief runs to their winter storage areas, where they deposited them and came back for more.

It was the best time I could remember in years and made me long for a pet. I'd given up the idea of having a cat because Ben said he was allergic to them. Of course, dogs in the city meant scooping poop off the sidewalk in quart-sized baggies before breakfast, which, when added to Ben's early morning diatribe, was more shit than I could take.

I shook off those thoughts, went inside, and showered in the tiny tin box with low water pressure. So much lake water and so little shower water. Must be three-inch pipes trying to pull the lake water up the hill.

After my drip-shower, I dressed and headed for town to scope out the locals and perhaps run into the Lake Goddess, the only other creature in the woods that interested me.

The Muskie Café sported a huge wooden board over its entrance with a painted fish on it. In fact, all the buildings seemed to have a fish fetish. I decided to go inside for coffee and a homemade sweet roll. When I opened the door, all heads turned, the row of mostly bearded men at the counter stared at me, and then they all turned back to their food. Every wall had at least four huge mounted fish on it, and I envisioned their heads turning too. *I've seen too many Geico commercials.*

A young waitress in a pink-and-white shirtwaist dress and a starched white apron, looking as crisp and retro as a WWII poster, came over to the booth to get my order. After she left, an older, heavy-set woman who walked with a limp joined me to ask if I was Alice Armand's niece. I told her I was and asked how she knew her. She said they had worked the church dinners every August.

"Your aunt was a fine woman, and she could make a raspberry preserve to die for, and of course all the kids loved her because she was always up to something crazy." The woman laughed. "She didn't have too much luck in the men department, but I don't think that bothered her, far as I could tell. Anyway, I'm glad I ran into you. Hadn't thought of Alice in a while."

And she was off, leaving me with secondhand images of salt-of-the-earth, jelly-making, child-hugging, man-hating Aunt Alice.

Through the window, I caught sight of the blond woman. *The Lake Goddess going into the drugstore.* What mundane items could a lake goddess possibly need from the drugstore? A refill on her magic potion to ensnare men's hearts?

I paid up and dashed out of the café. She was finishing up at the counter, talking to a young female clerk. She didn't seem to be buying anything and was already exiting the drugstore when I hit the street. I followed her to the post office. Why was I following her? I wasn't really following her. I needed to go to the post office too.

She entered the tiny building, and I hung back as if pretending to get my bearings, checking out the water company next door and the boat-motor repair shop. Having given it the appropriate amount of time to make my arrival seem coincidental, I entered.

"Warming up out your way?" the postmaster asked the woman.

"It is. And more loons seem to be on the lake this year. I always love their cry." The mystery woman's voice was deep and sensual, but no-nonsense. I could have listened to her for hours. Her golden hair was short and curly and worn close to her head, like a woman who participates in athletic events and has to keep her hair out of her eyes. She was forty, maybe, wearing khaki slacks, a V-neck, three-quarter-sleeved shirt, neatly tucked in, and a cognac leather belt that matched her shoes. *She has to be from out of town.* I was aware my thought was biased but then took up for myself. *Have I seen anyone else remotely that coordinated since I've been here? There you have it!* I told my politically correct self.

"Wife loves the loons too." The postmaster brightened when he talked to her. "Here you go. Take care."

"You too." The woman took her change, turned, and walked past me.

"Hi!" I said, immediately realizing that I sounded like a starstruck teenager.

She paused for a split second, looked into my eyes, smiled, and said, "Well, hello." And she left.

She might as well have said I'd won the lotto, because I was inexplicably happy.

The postmaster jolted me back to earth. "How can I help you?"

"Stamps. A dozen. Who's the lady who just said hello? I feel like I know her." I was lying, hoping for a name.

"That's the woman out on White Horse Point," he said, as if everyone knew that, and quickly gave me change.

"Oh, so she's a permanent resident." I was delighted for no apparent reason.

"'Bout as permanent as the rest of us." He laughed, and I hurried back outside and watched her retrace her steps. I casually followed her until I reached the center of town and the Muskie Café, where an elderly Swedish man intercepted me, causing me to lose sight of her.

"Hey, there, Alice Armand's niece! Are ya lookin' for company over a cup? Helen at the market told me you was here." He held the cafe door for me, and it was my second trip inside in only half an hour. But no one seemed to think that odd, because this time no one raised his head to look at me. My elderly escort introduced himself as Maynard Swensen.

"Me and my wife Wilma knew yer aunt and uncle real good," he said with that attractive Norwegian lilt.

He was a big-boned fellow with thin, sandy hair and soft, blue eyes that must have attracted the ladies back before the cataracts gave him an otherworldly stare. Despite his elderly appearance, his gnarled hands looked powerful. He was what people up North called "hard as wood."

When I asked about his wife, he laughed. "She was yust too sportin' for an ole horse like me, so we got unhitched."

"I guess that happens," I said, not wanting to dig deeper.

"Ya. Happened to your auntie too…cuz ole Yake, he done sneaked around with my wife."

"Oh, my gosh. I didn't know."

"Well, now ya do!" He gave a big, hearty laugh. "Now ya do," he repeated quietly and stared off into space, apparently lost in a different time. I didn't know what to say about his festering thorn of cuckolded love, other than to hope it would work itself out.

I told him I was glad he stopped to talk and that I was sure I'd see him again before the summer was over, and I paid for both our coffees, as familial penance on behalf of Uncle Jake, Rake-of-the-Lake.

"Lake brings that out in people," Maynard said, trailing behind me out the door. "Hot sun, cold beer, cool water lappin' up against ya, pine trees whisperin' to ya. Gets a lotta folks in trouble. Fact is, most people think the whole Point is haunted by love gone wrong."

Like a kid who'd just seen her parents having sex, I wanted to run away and think privately about what had happened. Uncle Jake running around on Aunt Alice—and with some lake woman in a town of 989 people, probably 789 back then—where everyone knew everyone. How embarrassing for Aunt Alice, but of course, in those days, women pretended everything was just fine.

❖

I'd no sooner pulled in at the cabin than a woman I assumed was Marney came sailing out of the white cabin's back door, the screen banging loudly behind her as she crossed the yard, arms outstretched. She was small in stature and decked out in peach tennies, peach bows, and peach fabric that blew in the wind and swooped around me like an out-of-control kite. When she hugged me, her heavily made-up face landed in the vicinity of my cleavage, and I immediately deemed her the lake elf. She apologized for not being here when I arrived, but, she paused to catch her breath, "I'm part of the committee getting ready for the church dinners."

Marney had a round, friendly face, lots of black curls, dark eyes, pink polish on her fingers and toes, and a happy demeanor that I envied, while at the same time found annoying. It was like bubbles. A few are fun, but a bottle full of them nearly chokes you.

She held me at arm's length, tilted her head up to look into my eyes, and quizzed me like a mother: Was I settled in? Did I have food? Was the bed comfortable? Did I know how to adjust the heat in case it got cold at night? *Finally, something that will loosen her grip on me.*

"I don't know how to work the heat," I said. She let go of me and barreled inside the cabin, with me behind her, where she searched for heating instructions in the silverware drawer with the intensity of a dog digging a hole, then waved them in the air with all the enthusiasm of someone who'd just discovered the Dead Sea Scrolls. "Fouuund them!"

She scanned the instructions quickly, then tinkered with the levers and valves on the pot-bellied stove, all while giving me a verbal tour of the lake.

"So we're in Ramona's cabin here, and then Ralph and I live next door in the white cabin. The red cabin is next, and it's ours too. We rent it out to different people all summer—rarely the same ones. You'll love the Robertsons, a mother and daughter who'll be coming up in a few weeks. They've always stayed at Jensen's but were so happy our red cabin came available. Then there's the old two-story cabin we rent out to local hunters and fishermen in the fall. That's a hoot! We practically have to take a hose to the place after they leave. Past that cabin is lots of woods, until you reach the far end of the horseshoe, where at night, you can see a light way out on the Point. Back in the woods is a cabin with thirty acres."

The stove belched and shook, and flames roared behind the glass door, threatening to leap out and ignite Marney's "peachedness." I tugged at her sleeve to pull her back from the flames, but she waved me off. "Ignore that!" she said, like the Great and Powerful Oz, and jumped back without a break in her monologue. "The former owner was a gorgeous, tall creature who used to own the entire cove but gradually sold it off, including the land that wraps around the Point farther east, into another cove where Jensen's sits, along with cabins they rent out." She took a deep breath. "Okay. This is the only knob you need to bother about. It's off now, but turn it up for warmer, down for cooler. Ramona says you just need to relax and unwind, and that ole writer's block will drown in the lake."

I started to refute the writer's block but decided it wasn't worth it. I made a mental note to kill Ramona instead. Marney scrounged two tickets to the church dinner from somewhere under her diaphanous get-up and slapped them into my palm. "Third week in August, so plan to come."

I thanked her for settling me in, and she beamed. "I'm just glad to have company. My husband Ralph is such a sphinx." She hugged me, and I had empathy for Ralph.

CHAPTER FOUR

The sun glittered through my bedroom window as I stretched and yawned, feeling I was in a place more luxurious than New York's Peninsula Hotel. I got my coffee and came back to bed, cuddled up in the quilt, and watched fish jump in the lake. It wasn't long before I heard a tap at the door and realized it was Marney, who wanted to know how I was doing and if I'd slept well. After a couple of exchanges, she launched into a monologue about life on the lake and how she and Ralph ended up here.

I made the excuse that I had to shower and get into town and suspected she wanted to ask why, but I had the door closed before she could.

On the drive in, I began creating ways to avoid her without insulting her. I was in town before I came up with a good plan.

I stopped in front of a tall, colorful totem pole growing up out of the sidewalk at the entrance of the Muskie Trading Post, where Native Americans sold shirts, blankets, and jewelry. I bought a loose-fitting, pale-green shirt with red ponies on it from Little Man, ironically an overly tall Ojibwe Indian, and he liked my choice. He said the shirt was covered in the Lac La Croix ponies that were once indigenous to his tribe.

"Are the ponies still around here?" I asked.

"No, almost extinct. Some in Canada."

"Do you know anything about White Horse Point?

"The Point is haunted." He spoke in a matter-of-fact tone.

"Who haunts it?"

"The story goes that the horsewoman, Angelique, was in love with someone she couldn't have. There was talk about him being her groom, and someone else said her farrier. She died never knowing love, and now she's back constantly looking for him." The way he said it made me think that was his official tourist spiel.

"Do you believe that?"

He paused, and I remained silent. "I believe it is a place where spirits come in."

I wanted to ask if he'd seen a spirit there, but he walked away, clearly having said all he intended.

Angelique. What are the odds of that name popping up again? I locked my packages in the car before walking two blocks toward the post office and the water company. My mind replayed what Little Man had said about the Point being haunted, and he'd called the woman Angelique, the name of the woman on the plane who'd disappeared. A brisk breeze ran up my arms and sent a chill down my spine. Had I seen Angelique? How would that be possible?

The town appeared to be less planned and more sprung up. A house with a tiny yard filled with wildflowers that stood taller than a ten-year-old child was sandwiched between Muskie Boat-Motor Repair, with its gasoline fumes and motor noises, and the Muskie Water Department, which was one small room with a lady at the counter who greeted me as I entered. She was a pretty, middle-aged, solidly built woman with blond hair, blue eyes, and a too-tight dress of blue and white flowers.

I introduced myself and said I didn't want to bother Marney, but "I found a minnow in my tap water." I spoke very calmly when actually I wanted to scream a fucking fish flew out of my faucet, and it was still breathing, and I could have swallowed the damned thing if I'd been drinking. As it was, I put the offending fish in a coffee cup, took it down to the lake, and threw him back in, which was a humanitarian act I didn't want to have to repeat.

The woman, her blond hair roped in a halo around her head, said crisply, "You just need a tighter mesh screen on the end of your lake pipe…that's a handyman job. I'll see if one of the boys can do it, and I'll send him by. Both of them look about the same, except one's bald and one's *real* bald." She laughed. "Good workers, both of 'em. They do odd jobs for guests in the cabins. About the minnows…just scoop 'em out. They won't kill you. Old Maynard eats them." She laughed, but I wasn't sure she was joking.

I was beginning to understand what customer service sounded like up North with women like this one at the helm, who, despite her jolly attitude, looked like she might smack me if I continued to make a big deal out of a small fish.

As I drove back to the cabin, I thought about Minnow-Munching Maynard chomping live fish in his drinking water and started to gag. I made a mental note to check the sink's filtering system. If a minnow made its way out of the sink faucet, what the hell was the system filtering, crawdads and leeches? *I've got to buy bottled water.*

No sooner had I pulled into the drive than the curtains separated at Marney-the-Lake-Elf's place. She was poised for a visit, so I dashed across the lawn with the speed and intensity of someone either headed for the bathroom or a stove fire. Marney receded into her cabin as I hit the back door. I had to find a way to let her know I needed space.

Too late. She was on the steps, and I had started to rise to new levels of anxiety just as she extended her hands, offering me a plastic plate of fresh fish right out of the frying pan.

"We were having fish, so I thought you should too. Can't come to the cabin and not have fish. Walleyed pike. The best," she said, and I thanked her profusely.

Nice lady brings you dinner, and you're ready to kill her for invading your space. You're a dick, Taylor, I said to myself. Let the fuck up.

❖

I sat on the enclosed porch after dark with the lights off and watched the moonlight on the mirror-like water. It was so bright it lit up the white stand of birch trees at the edge of the hill, before the land sloped down into the lake. The birch trees' snowy skin peeled back and hung loosely off the trunk, daring me to pull the bark free and write on it like parchment, or make a toy canoe out of it, like I'd done as a child. But too much bark removal would leave the trees vulnerable to disease, so I resisted. The light on their white trunks was magical.

Suddenly I spotted something white on the lake, moving away from the Point toward me but still several hundred yards away. The shape was so odd, like a giant amoeba expanding and contracting, that it was almost scary. I grabbed the binoculars, and the contrast of the dark lake against this white object moving closer and closer through the water was surreal. It wasn't a boat. I stood up, focusing the lens. *It's a white horse, and it's paddling across the water.* And on its back sat a woman riding bareback across the lake, her bare legs visible beneath her white nightshirt, the collar up, and her blond hair in the moonlight making her look like a model in a Ralph Lauren ad. Silent ripples formed behind her, as she and the horse swam closer, and closer, then away from the shore but across from my cabin, circling, looking, then heading back to the Point. *It's the Lake Goddess.* I immediately wondered if she was crazy, but I was captivated by her nonetheless.

She's like a trip back in time, where the water and the fog were backdrops for mystical power. She looks powerful, I thought. It must be the white horse that makes her appear so strong. But what the hell is she doing?

CHAPTER FIVE

The old house phone gave off a loud, metallic clang that startled me. Ramona was on the line checking to see how I was doing and if I'd heard any lake gossip she needed to be made aware of. Like all good publicists, information was currency, and by those standards, Ramona was rich.

"It's beautiful here and so relaxing, but everyone's a bit off. This nice old guy, Maynard Swensen, invited me to the 'stuffed-fish café,'" I said, casting aspersions on the coffee shop with so many mounted fish. "He told me Uncle Jake had an affair with his wife."

"That is such old news. He needs to get over it." Ramona sounded disgusted.

"You knew that? Why didn't you tell me?"

"Now, how would that topic ever come up?"

"Marney's like Velcro. You didn't warn me about her. And then there's the Lake Goddess. She rode a white horse bareback into the lake in her nightshirt at midnight, paddled over toward the cabin, and then went back to the Point."

"That's odd, but it speaks to a certain talent—bareback in the middle of the cove at dark."

"Maybe I should go back to New York. I could be nuts by fall and dead by winter."

Saying "nuts" reminded me of the chipmunks, and I moved toward the porch to feed them while we chatted. Instantly I was yanked back, losing my balance, as the phone cord wrapped around my neck, nearly strangling me before I managed to plop down in a chair. "Holy shit. I was nearly decapitated by the fucking wall phone!"

Ramona ignored my drama and remained focused on the woman in the lake. "I didn't know anyone was on the Point after Angelique died. Maybe she's a transient."

"Transient!" I laughed. "I don't know any transients who own horses and hang around waiting for thirty-below-zero winters. Transients are on foot in places with coconuts and sand," I said, rubbing my neck where the cord had lashed it.

"You know, I bet that's Angelique's niece. She was a little kid the last time I saw her. Was this woman pretty?"

"Gorgeous." The adjective just popped out.

"Must be the niece. What are you doing to relax?"

"I have two free tickets to the church dinner. Want to fly in?"

"The altar would melt. When you're through with the church dinners, write something, will you?" That was Ramona's version of "Talk to you soon." She hung up.

Finally I concocted a tall tale to break the cycle of Marney visits, telling her Ramona had called, which was true, and that I was on deadline this week, which was sort of true, and this meant I would be sleeping during the day and working late into the night while it was quiet. Marney looked dejected but said she understood. So now I had to make good on my lie or simply pace around the cabin all night.

For the first time since I'd arrived, I pulled my laptop out of my duffel. The internet was working, but my email was scant. When Ben and I divorced, most of the people I knew were his friends, and when they sided with him, I destroyed their contact information, blocked them on Facebook, and basically cut off the world. It didn't matter that I knew they sided with him because he was quick to donate money to their charity events or help them with attorney advice. I still felt like I'd been thrown over the side of the boat for lack of anything they needed.

I opened the Word document to the beginning of the story and stared for several minutes at the words I'd written two years ago. They no longer seemed right, and I sat there contemplating that fact. After a while my fingers, apparently tired of my brain's inability to direct them, decided to do something on their own. They typed, "I feel like I'm just waiting." I stared at the sentence as if it were automatic writing and being directed by an alien presence.

What am I waiting for? What? I don't know how long I sat there, but the scratching on the window screen in the bedroom off the living room snapped me back to the present. The cabin was built on two-foot cinderblocks, to keep the logs off wet winter ground, and the windows were intentionally constructed neck-high from ground level, to keep people and animals out, so what was scratching on the screen? Whatever it was, it would have to be tall. A bear! Is it a bear? I grabbed the phone to call Marney, but the shadow outside spoke.

"It's Ralph, from next door."

I put the phone back in the cradle and tried to settle my pounding heart.

Cracking open the screen door, I saw him rounding the corner of the house to the back steps. "You scared me to death!"

"I'm so sorry." He hugged me, reeking of so much aftershave I thought he'd fallen down in a drugstore. "I just saw your light on in the living room and didn't know if you were okay." He put his hand on the screen-door handle to hold the door open.

I explained that I'd told Marney I was going to be working nights.

"Oh, I'm so sorry. Marney didn't tell me. We kind of pass in the night any more. So you're a writer." He uttered the dreaded phrase that meant he intended to park his short, wide, middle-aged frame on my doorstep and maybe tell me how he wanted to be a writer too, so I stepped out of the house to keep Ralph and the mosquitoes from entering. He must have mistaken that for some sort of personal interest, because he came forward instead of backing up. I kept going, taking a firm step toward him, saying, "I have got to get back to work. Thanks for checking on me."

And that's when Ralph went airborne, getting his feet tangled up as he stepped backward off the porch, losing his balance, arms flailing, his torso banging into the thin pipe railing, and finally his forehead smashing onto the cement. *Oh, my God he's bleeding like the subway woman. I'm being stalked by head wounds! Well, I'm not turning my good shirt into a tourniquet!*

I ran into the kitchen, grabbed sheets of paper towels, dampened them, and applied a compress to his head. "Sit down right here on the steps," I ordered him, and he obeyed, his rumpled Bermuda shorts and jungle-flowered Tommy Bahama shirt collapsing into a heap, making him look like a human laundry bag. "I'll get Marney."

"No! No! I'm fine. Don't bother her. She'll take care of me when I get home." And with that he staggered off into the dark. I sat down and contemplated Ralph racing across the lawn holding his bloody head. What would he tell Marney, and what would she think? And what was he doing over here in the dead of night? Did she even know that he'd left the cabin?

I was sitting on the enclosed porch holding my laptop as if it might start to write for me again, when I saw a faint light on the Point and grabbed the binoculars that always sat on the window ledge. I adjusted the focus, and a large campfire became visible, casting a bright glow over the blond woman sitting beside it. Two large dogs, one on each side of her, kept watch. Even from this distance, I could see the light bounce off her white slacks. Little Man, the tall Indian man from the trading post, was seated nearby, and he seemed to be performing some kind of ceremony, offering something up toward the sky with both hands.

For a moment, I thought a taller woman in riding clothes was sitting beside them, and I was sad that I couldn't join them. Then

I asked myself why I would think that. *So you want to squat in the woods by a fire and be bitten by a thousand mosquitoes?* I looked through the binoculars again, and the image of the second woman quickly proved to be smoke, or fog, or nothing at all.

Despite Little Man's presence, the blond woman seemed to be talking to someone who wasn't there. Or maybe she was talking to herself. That was spooky. And then, as if she knew I was watching, she looked directly at me. It was more than a glance in my direction. She literally stared right at me, my eyes connecting with hers, which I knew was completely impossible from this distance and in the dark. I froze, wondering if she really knew I was here looking at her, and was she trying to pull me toward her? "And how is that even possible when I'm looking through fucking binoculars?" I said out loud and quickly put the binoculars down as if they were possessed. But regardless, I could see her looking at me.

That idea so unnerved me that I slept with a pillow over my head. Alone in the woods during the day was delightful, but alone in the woods at night was eerie. *How does that woman live way out on the Point all alone?*

❖

The next day, Marney came over dragging Ralph, who had a gauze bandage wrapped around his head at a forty-five-degree angle, making him look like a hospital pirate, and I was unsure how this encounter was going to play out. Maybe Marney didn't know her husband was scratching on windows late at night until this happened, and now she wanted an accounting of our late-night rendezvous.

She bustled up to me and seemed about to cry. I waited. She took in a deep breath and said in adult baby-talk, "Look at my poor Ralphie." I cringed, which she took to mean I understood how horribly hurt he was, when in fact, it was just that an adult talking baby talk, even if they were addressing a baby, was like nails on a chalkboard.

"He fell off the dock and hit his widdle head." She pursed her lips, becoming an adult toddler.

Ralph didn't look at me, and I managed not to grin.

"He was trying to save some silly boy who swam over from one of Jensen's rental cabins drunk and exhausted, and my Ralphie was a hero." She beamed and hugged him, and he seemed to enjoy the attention. I glanced down and realized the top step still had some of Ralph's blood on it. I slid my foot over, to cover the worst spot, and reminded myself to hose off the incriminating stain.

Ralph must have left my place, gone down to the lake, waded into the water to get the blood off him, and then had to find a way to weave his wet clothes into his alibi.

I reached for a phrase that would ring true. "I hope you heal quickly."

Marney assured me that, under her care, he would, and she said they'd only dropped by to say if I had any odd jobs I needed Ralph's help with, they would have to wait for the next couple of days, because Ralph was incapacitated. Looking at him, I wanted to say he was the last man I'd call to air up an inner tube, but I just nodded, indicating I understood he was out of commission.

And they were off, bouncing back across the yard, bumping into each other playfully, like two tethered balloons, and disappearing into the white cabin.

❖

That night, I heard another sound on the lake side, as if someone was moving through the pinecones. I headed out the door, vowing that if it was Ralph, trying for an amorous double dip, I'd kill him.

Instead, it was the woman in white, the Lake Goddess, at the water's edge, where she dismounted and stood in the moonlight looking up at the cabin, apparently checking on something. She was startlingly beautiful, and I was afraid she would disappear, so I hurried out the door and scrambled over the embankment and down to the water to greet her, losing my footing on rocks, pinecones, and underbrush and skidding into view on my butt. Embarrassed, I got up and dusted myself off.

The woman looked up at me, and I thought she was the most exquisite creature I'd ever seen. *Why is someone that beautiful in the woods, in the water, in my soul?* I caught myself. *In my soul?* The high drama of that thought nearly made me laugh.

"Don't you sleep?" Her intonation sounded more like an invitation not to sleep.

I found myself answering in the same tone. "Don't you have a boat?"

The woman paused and then laughed, seemingly at something beyond my comment, something she'd remembered. "My aunt asked me to stop by and have a look," she said, oblivious to her surroundings and staring directly at me.

"And what are you supposed to look at?"

"You," she said. Her eyes moved up and down the length of me. "Tall, trim, nice broad shoulders, lovely hands, great eyes."

She glanced up at the sky, talking to someone or something. "Happy?" Then she cocked her head to one side and gave me a sparkling smile, and I smiled back. "I do love the smile," she said in a tone that was unmistakably provocative.

"Would you mind telling me your name?"

"Levade. It rhymes with odd," she said, letting me know her reputation.

"Of course." The words escaped before I had polished them. "Isn't that a horse jump or something?"

"It's one of the movements a horse can be trained to execute. My mother let my aunt name me."

Strange sounds coming through the white cabin's windows rescued me from any more awkward attempts at conversation. It sounded like a struggle, or a mugging, or God knows what, so we both focused in that direction. I was about to scurry up the embankment and intervene when, completely embarrassed, I realized Marney and Ralph must be having sex.

"Oh, no, it's the neighbors fornicating." I made a silly face, and Levade laughed. "Let this be a reminder to both of us that the animal grunts, moans, and gasps of lovemaking are embarrassing secondhand, so always try to be the one having sex, not hearing sex."

"Thank you for that advice."

She suppressed a giggle, and I loved that I could make her laugh.

"Why, at this very moment, while I am trying to impress my guest, must Ralph and Marney broadcast their lovemaking play by play, and leave the windows open?" I whispered.

At that very moment, Ralph launched into repetitive ecstasy. "Oh baby, oh baby, oh baby, ooooh baby!"

It almost sounded like the background track to an old fifties tune. Finally, an amazingly robust grunt emanated from Ralph, a glass-shattering scream from Marney, and then, mercifully, silence.

"Damn. I'm glad that's over," I said, shaking my head. "'Oh, baby' was just about to become permanently lodged in my brain between 'It's a Small World' and 'Felice Navidad.'"

"Sounds like they're having more fun than we are," Levade teased. Those words were like a caress, and I felt oddly shy.

"All I can say is that Ralph has apparently solved his marital dilemmas. He and Marney are no longer ships passing in the night, but more like a maritime merger."

Why couldn't I have someone to make love to? And when I did have someone, why did that particular activity never seem very satisfying?

"Cabins were created for Ralph-and-Marney moments," Levade said sweetly. Then, without so much as a good-bye, she led her horse back into the water, shoulder deep, floated onto his back, and they paddled back onto the lake toward the Point. I watched until they disappeared. I wanted to go with her. I wanted her to keep looking at me and never stop.

❖

That night I dreamed I was in my bed and awoke to see Levade standing on the shoreline. She dismounted and walked up to my cabin and into my bedroom. She shrugged off her white gown and stood naked, smiling at me seductively, and I had an intense desire to hold her. She somehow knew that and slid in beside me under the sheets, then wrapped herself around me, and in the next moment she was kissing me in the most erotic way, rubbing her body against mine. Then she was inside me, and I was nearly orgasmic—hot, and thrashing, and wet. I awoke in a sweat, kicking the covers off, and jumped out of bed as if she were really in there with me.

"Wow!" I said out loud to no one. How long had it been since I'd had a sexual dream about being taken by a man? *How long has it been since I've had a sexual dream, period? Why am I having an erotic dream about that woman?*

Chapter Six

I whispered into the phone, though no one could hear me but Ramona, "Ralph came by one night unannounced and scratched on my screen like a rutting stag. He fell on the porch steps and hit his head and then refused to let me call Marney, because I don't think she knew he was on the prowl."

"Ralph on the prowl?" Ramona laughed.

"Then that woman, Levade, the one you think is Angelique's niece, floated up on shore like an angel on a white horse and then floated off."

"What did you say to her?"

"I said, don't you have a boat?"

"No wonder she left. That was just damned weird. You don't know her. She probably thought you were making fun of her. People up North are different. Maybe she can't afford a boat."

"You're overthinking it. It's been a week, and I've gotten jack done. It's the same as New York—people doing weird shit, talking too much. It's like everyone here just has their mind on getting laid." *And, it's starting to rub off on me with all my sex dreams of late.* "In fact, Marney and Ralph had screaming-ass sex with their windows open, and I had to hear all of it, including, the 'Ooooh, baby' aria."

Ramona laughed loudly. "Good for Marney! The woods will do that to you. It's as if you're on another planet and you'll never see these people again, so why not take off your clothes and fuck like fish. Are you writing?"

"Yes," I said, which was true, despite it being only one new sentence.

"Do I need to come see you? I miss the cabin. Great times, and very studly men, if memory serves."

"God, no. That's all I need is you here. I'm busy writing."

Around noon, I heard a polite knock at the back door, and, as if Ramona had conjured him, a handsome, muscular man, in his early forties, with piercing blue eyes, who was small in stature by Viking standards, introduced himself as Frank, the Muskie Champion. He wondered out loud if I'd like to pay him to take me on a guided tour of the area by boat, see some of the wildlife and his taxidermy shop. He was dark-haired, and he moved with the physical confidence of a man who knew he'd accomplished something in life.

"Most people see only the part of the lake they live on. Muskie Lake is eight miles long, with more than a hundred coves and all kinds of beautiful wildlife back off the shore." I glanced at his shirt, and the ball cap he was wearing that proclaimed him Muskie Champion three years running. He noticed I was checking out his clothing billboard. "I've caught the largest muskies in Minnesota. One was over five feet long and weighed more than sixty-five pounds, a monster for a freshwater fish. I'd be happy to show it to you. A lot of men want me to take them on muskie expeditions. I charge them and make them travel blindfolded in the boat, so they can't steal my fishing spots." He cracked his knuckles for emphasis and gave me a winning grin.

"How much?" I asked.

"A hundred dollars for the day."

"Can we go now?" I was sold when he mentioned getting to see animals back in the woods. Further, I was making it a point not to delay any new experience. He seemed delighted we were going immediately—instant income, I assumed.

Frank's big, yellow, fiberglass boat was the cabin cruiser of lake boats, with sonar and radar equipment and big, leather armchair seats. He put the motor in full throttle, and we thrashed across the open waters, then suddenly slowed as he hit a lever and the motor quickly tilted, lifting the propeller into the air as we coasted over a wide stretch of sand only a foot below the surface.

"Lot of guys come out here, don't know where the sandbars are, sheer a pin on their first time out, and have to be towed. Kind of puts a kink in their macho." He grinned and I laughed. He waved me over to look at his elaborate dashboard and tapped the cover of the dial, focusing me. "Spot we're on now is about 160-feet deep." He showed me how the depth meter worked and how he could use it, not only to navigate but to find the best fishing grounds.

"Only the sheriff's boat has equipment even close to this. Sam uses it to rescue tourists. A few have drowned out here because they don't understand drop-offs. You can be walking along sure-footed for a hundred yards off the shoreline, chatting away, and the next step you're in Beijing." He grinned at me again. "You take in water and drown."

"So where are these little animals you were going to show me?" I changed the subject, not wanting to think I was sailing across the surface of bloated tourist bodies.

Frank whipped the boat into a cove in dramatic fashion, sending a spray of water into the air. He shut down the motor in an instant, and the water dragging behind us made a huge whooosh before slapping up on the shore "Beer?" he asked, pulling one from the ice chest, his eyes focused on the land. We sat in total silence for about ten minutes.

A rotund skunk waddled through the woods. Then along the water's edge, I spotted a creature that looked like a beaver, and it caught Frank's eye too.

"Beavers burrow in the lake banks because the water's too deep for dam-building. They build their dams in ponds where the water's shallow."

Around sundown, Frank lifted the motor, and we drifted through the narrows, a shallow, skinny part of the lake known to have patches of quicksand beneath the surface. Along the banks, the narrows were home to six-foot-tall stands of cattails with their brown, fuzzy, hot-dog shaped tops. Giant water lilies covered the lake's surface, and here and there remaining stalks of wild rice protruded from the water, having obviously missed the harvest.

"You ever find yourself in quicksand, don't struggle," Frank said. "Look around and try to find even the tiniest cattails or twigs, something you can get hold of, and slowly, no matter how long it takes, try to get your feet up and parallel with the water's surface. Getting dark, so I'll take you by my shop before we call it a day."

We navigated out of the narrows and blew through the water, then slowed for the occasional fishing boat. "If you have to cross in front of them, slow down and do it as far away as you can, and at a ninety-degree angle, because a small boat can cross that angle of chop, but a big parallel wake will rock them side to side and tip them over." I was impressed with all the things Frank knew.

We pulled into his dock where the shoreline ran right up to the back steps of his cabin. From the boat, I could see an array of taxidermy animals through the picture windows, the bears with their paws in the air as if waving to us. They stood like frozen sentinels watching for him to come home.

His door was unlocked, and we walked into his cabin that could have been a museum exhibit on north-woods animals and their habitat. I pivoted 360 degrees. I'd never seen so many dead, but preserved, animals. It's Country Bear Jamboree purgatory, I thought, but I couldn't help but walk around and touch their fur. Every animal was placed in a staging area with tree branches, logs, and rocks surrounding them, giving the sense that they were still alive in the woods. *And this is the guy's house*? It would be like sleeping in a pet cemetery.

"Deer, bear, wolf, fox, muskies, of course—there's my sixty-five-pounder. And otters, muskrat, beaver, porcupine, wild hog—anything that ever lived up here." Frank was still in tour-guide mode.

I glanced at three fluffy, foxlike creatures. "They're so darling and so lifelike, I can't stand to see them dead. What are they?"

"You sound like my wife." He chuckled good-naturedly. "Taxidermy wasn't her thing either. She died a year ago, and I really miss her. I don't like being alone."

"I'm so sorry. How did she die?"

"No one really knows." He gave me an ironic grin. "I don't like to talk about it."

"I understand." I was feeling uncomfortable for no particular reason. "Well, it's been a great day. Thank you." I instinctively checked for a door that would take me out of the cabin and onto the road.

"I didn't mean to cut you off when you asked about her. I'm sure I'll marry again. You know, I bought her a lot of expensive clothes, and I saved them all. I want to marry someone her size so they don't go to waste. You're about her size."

My body went cold, the way any woman's body temperature shifts dramatically when she senses danger.

"Well, it takes more than a pant size to make a marriage work. I'm still getting over my divorce. I need to get back home. I'm waiting for a business call. Mind if we drive?" I paid him in cash, not wanting him to have a check with my name and New York address on it.

"It's your day."

We walked to his truck and climbed in. I clutched the door handle and made note of every twist in the road on the drive to the cabin. Just beneath that veneer of politeness, something about him was chilling. I mentally moved him to that column of people who "aren't quite right" and should be avoided.

When he pulled into the drive at my cabin, the sun was about to set. I hopped out, thanking him as I moved quickly to the cabin door.

"Let's do it again!" he sang out, and I didn't answer but just waved good-bye.

What had possessed me to go out on the lake with a man I didn't know anything about, simply because he'd shown up at my door wearing a freaking logo shirt that said he catches big fish? No one even knew I was out there with him. *He could have thrown me in the fricking quicksand bog!*

CHAPTER SEVEN

The visit to Frank's cabin troubled me so much that the following day, I drove to town to see about buying a shotgun and a couple of boxes of shells at the hardware store. The entire "Frank experience" reminded me of how vulnerable I was. Living in New York, every woman is on alert all the time about her surroundings, and where she is after dark, and who's in the elevator with her. When the fast-food woman was pushed in front of the subway train, while none of us could stop it, people were there to take immediate action. In the woods, you're lulled into a sense of tranquility, and when something happens, no one's around. There was certainly no one in my cabin I could run to for help, not even a dog. So a gun seemed logical.

The rifles and shotguns were lined up on the wall behind the clerk, their stocks seated in wooden cradles and their barrels pointing skyward like steel soldiers. I asked a few questions about how hard they kicked, having heard the recoil of some guns can bruise your shoulder, and which gun in particular would be best suited for a woman my size.

"What are you intending to shoot?" The clerk, a wiry lady in her fifties with frizzy hair and an infectious grin, asked me point-blank.

"Whatever comes at me in the night."

"I should tell my husband that." We both laughed, and she introduced herself as Gladys Williamson. "You know a 'blast and scatter' is going to be your best bet, if you're just warding off animals. I'd say this 12-gauge, and it's got a padded stock that would probably be more comfortable for you."

"I'm sure I won't have to fire it." I took the shotgun from her and ran my hand over the sleek polished wood, keeping my fingerprints off the steel that had a beautiful scene of deer in the woods etched into it. "This will be fine," I said. "I took a tour of the lake with this Frank fellow. You know him?"

"Sure do," she said emphatically, and immediately busied herself writing up my ticket and then straightening the boxes of bullets on the back counter, signaling conversation closed.

"Who's the local sheriff?" I asked as I wrote a check.

"Sam Lindhurst. And his office is right across the street and down a block."

I thanked her, left the store, locked the gun in my car, turned around, and there she was.

"You bought a gun. Do you know how to use it?" Levade asked calmly, and her blue eyes completely captivated me.

"Hello! Every idiot in the woods has one, so it can't be that hard. Anyway, I'm on the way to the sheriff's office to see if he'll give me a lesson, so I can avoid shooting myself in the foot." *My God, she is strange, and so gorgeous.*

"I think you're smarter than that." She gave me her beautiful smile. "Just remember that a few hours at a shooting range is fine if you're thinking of scaring off animals, but if you're thinking it will scare people away, it takes a lot more. Please be careful. Don't take any more tours of the lake, okay?" She seemed genuinely concerned yet didn't wait for my answer. She merely walked away and got in her Jeep. How did she know I toured the lake with Frank? I'd just told Gladys, but she'd had little time to inform her. Frank must have let her know himself, and why would he do that? I watched her drive off wondering if she was crazy, or eccentric, or prescient, or just simply unnerving.

I headed for Sam's office. He sat behind a battered metal school desk that held his name plate and an old telephone. I liked him right away. He had a nice gray handlebar mustache and twinkly eyes, reminding me of Sam Waterston, if Sam Waterston were ten years younger and fifty pounds heavier.

"I wondered if I could pay you to give me a couple of shooting lessons."

He took his feet down off the desk and rose to greet me with a mannerly handshake. "Someone in particular you'd like to shoot?"

"No. I divorced him."

Sam grinned and agreed to meet me at a practice spot out in the woods in half an hour.

"How big's the sheriff's department?"

"You're looking at it. Me and maybe two ole boys who volunteer. When I leave, I just put a note on the door telling people where they can find me. Most of the time they don't want to find me."

❖

Sam gave me directions to the wooded area north of town known to hunters as a target-practice zone; the trees could bear witness to that, each sporting dozens of holes and lacerations. Sam picked up a few rusty cans off the ground, set them on a stump, and we started in.

I got the hang of loading and shooting and learned the safety tips pretty quick. Sam was a friendly, no-nonsense guy, and we worked for only about an hour.

"We hardly ever have tourists buy guns and practice shooting as part of their vacation." He let the remark hang.

"To tell you the truth, I'm on the lake alone, and it's just an insurance policy."

"Well, a lot of things look dangerous at first, but they're not always, so the secret is to think before you shoot, but don't think so long that you wish you'd shot." We both laughed. I tried to pay him, but he said "protect and serve" was part of his job, and it seemed like that's what he'd just done.

I felt secure now with my training and my new friend, Sam the sheriff. In fact, I was feeling so good that I headed back to town to Gus's tavern. I'd been told that bars up North were more family oriented than drinking establishments in the South. People gathered in a tavern to talk and watch football and gossip.

A short and battered ship's door led into a room so dark I had to stop and let my eyes adjust. Several men were at the bar, and two big-boned women were seated at a small table. I sat on a barstool and ordered a cabernet, while everyone in the bar visually examined me. No matter where I went, people stopped to take a look, like dogs sniffing the butt of a new arrival. I assumed they were checking me out to decide if it was okay for me to stay.

Gus, the owner, swabbed the bar top with his left hand and plopped my wine down with his right. The size of the wineglass was reminiscent of a medieval goblet. A big, athletic-looking, young woman in jeans and a dark-blue T-shirt with a navy insignia was serving other patrons.

Leaning into one wiry-looking guy, she warned, "He'll get you in trouble, Tony." She seemed to be referencing someone not in attendance.

The bald-headed man replied, "I've been in so much trouble all my life, it doesn't feel good if I'm not! Skol!" He lifted his glass in a toast to his apparently troubled life.

Other men chimed in. "Skol!"

She moved on, obviously tired of trying to teach pigs to sing.

With the tourist season, they were pretty busy, and I assumed they made most of their money in the summer. The men were raucous and joking with one another. One thin, gristly old man talked about a fish that got away. "She was so big she just broke my line and spit the hook back at me, then flipped that big sleek body in the air and took off. She would've broken all records."

"You sure you're not talking about a woman?" Gus, his big belly bouncing, injected himself into the conversation, apparently believing it was his job to keep people talking so they'd keep drinking. They both laughed.

The woman in the navy T-shirt had moved behind the bar, and she put a second glass of wine in front of me. "On me. Name's Kay. Welcome to the woods." I thanked her. "I live on the opposite side of the lake from you, but I can see the lights along the cove from my place, and it's nice to have so many cabins lit up this summer."

Gus immediately jumped in. "You the lady from New York? We don't get fancy New Yorkers often." I explained I used to come up to this lake as a kid, but he was already working on his not-from-here descriptor. "Another drink, Fancy Pants?"

"I just put one in front of her, Gus." Kay gave me an eye-roll as if to say men are clueless.

"So you know everybody around here," I said to Gus.

"Oh, ya."

"What's the story about the woman on the Point?" I asked.

"Well, let's see if I got all the names right. Psycho Psychic, Lady of the Loons, Horse's ass, A roll in the bay—"

Another man seated at the bar, clearly three sheets to the wind, guffawed and slurred his words. "Better watch what yer sayin', or she run you over with that horse!"

Kay shot me a look that seemed to say she could function as the bouncer if things got out of hand.

"Her name is Levade," I said, irritated at Gus's disparaging her and aware that I was feeling the buzz from the second glass of wine.

"Knew it started with an *L*." Gus paused. "Don't matter. You can call her anything, and she'll come." He laughed, and a couple of men joined in.

The anger shot up into my head like an ice cream headache. A scruffy, pot-bellied bar owner trashing a woman's reputation for a few laughs from a bunch of locals.

"Well, thanks for being a protector of the female gender," I said, raising my glass in a mock toast. "To Mr. Bar Wiper, who smells like a diaper, so much in demand he dates his right hand."

The men at the bar whooped and hollered and slapped the scarred, lacquered bar top. I tossed my money down on the counter and stalked out, as Kay gave me a thumbs-up.

Admittedly, had I not been a little high, I wouldn't have said that. In fact, I had no idea why I was defending a woman I barely knew. Maybe I was defending all women.

Maynard stepped out of the bar behind me, and I hadn't even realized he was in there.

"Gus ain't a bad fella, ya know. Yust been in the dark too long." He chuckled as he guided me to the curb, took a thermos of coffee out of his truck, and poured me a cup, while I leaned up against the hood. He didn't even mention I was mildly drunk or that I'd insulted Muskie citizen number 574. He just picked up where we'd left off.

"Ever since we had coffee, I thought about those days. Used to fish off the Point, and sometimes I'd watch Angelique work those white horses out on the beach. Seems like there was different ones. I was fishin' the old log bed for bass right off her dock, and I could see your auntie over there sometimes by moonlight, the two of 'em yust playin' with the horses like two young girls. That Angelique, she could make a horse tap-dance and sing the 'Star Spangled Banner.' Said she took her horses to this place where only white horses can go. Don't know if that's true, but it sounds real pretty."

I drank the coffee. "Tell me about this Frank guy. Seems like he's the star of the town, with all his fishing trophies."

"He's got skills and he's got demons. After his wife died, he left town for a while, but this was her home, and their home together, so he's come back. Don't think ya have any need of him." Maynard made me drink a second cup of coffee and patted my arm with his big, gnarled hand. "Ya drive slow home, ya?"

"Oh, ya," I said, thinking, my God, I've become a drunken Norwegian.

CHAPTER EIGHT

The story I'd begun writing two years ago in New York, and brought with me to the cabin, was about a man who was stalking his ex-wife because he believed her sexual forays were making a fool of him, even though they were no longer married. Meanwhile, the ex-wife was desperately looking for love but unclear what love looked like. *How can she find something she can't articulate, or recognize even if she sees it?* I pondered that question.

The house phone clanged.

"So how's it going?" Ramona asked.

"I was about to write *War And Peace,* Volume II, when you rang."

"I'll hang up, for God's sake!"

"No! I'll get back to it. I've seen some inspiring backdrops, if that makes you feel better. I took a tour of the lake with this really weird guy who knows all about the woods. The creepiest part was that his cabin is full of dead animals—he's a taxidermist."

"That's Frank Tinnerson! I had no idea he was still up there. Stay away from him. Everyone on the lake knows he killed his wife and had her dogs stuffed."

"What?! Those were dogs?"

"Pomeranians." Ramona was talking distractedly to someone who was obviously standing in her office doorway, and for a minute she tried to carry on two conversations, finally ending mine. "I've got to take care of this. Sorry. Marney can fill you in, but just don't be alone with him."

She hung up, and I immediately headed to Marney's. She was wearing a flowing pink, silk robe and fuzzy house slippers with floppy, golf-ball-sized poodle heads on each toe, giving me Frank-flashbacks. Her hair was in curlers, the kind I hadn't seen outside an old five and dime store in thirty years. She was delighted to see me, despite my having shunned her for a few days.

"The whole town knows Frank murdered his wife, but no one talks about it," Marney said, serving me tea and cookies. They were gingerbread and homemade, so I was beginning to warm up to chats with her.

Marney's white cabin was white inside as well as out. And every wall contained knickknack shelves with salt-and-pepper shakers in the shape of animals kissing. Pink ceramic, salt-and-pepper pigs kissing, black and white cows kissing, rodents, snakes, teapots, all ceramic, all salt-and-pepper shakers, and all kissing. Before I could comment, Marney explained, "Love is the salt and pepper of life!"

"Unless you have high blood pressure," I teased.

"Making love lowers your blood pressure," she confided in a whisper.

I had flashbacks of shrieking Marney and grunting Ralph having sex, but they were now two little ceramic salt-and-pepper hippos, which made me realize I'd traveled too far down the spice rack.

I shifted gears. "So Frank wasn't tried?"

"He wasn't even arrested. He said it was an accident and that he was heartbroken. Frank and his wife, her name was Dolores, fought all the time, I can tell you that. She was real pretty, with long black hair. In fact she looked a little bit Indian. I always thought Ojibwe, but Frank of course had to say she was European. Sometimes she'd show up in town with bruises, and she'd say she was clumsy and had an accident. But I heard she told someone that if she died, they should know that he killed her. The woods protects a lot of strange people."

"What about the woman on the Point?" I always managed to switch to that topic because she was my mind magnet, constantly pulling my thoughts in her direction.

"Speaking of strange people!" She laughed. "I don't know her, she keeps to herself, but her aunt was a famous equestrian. And she had these white horses she trained and traveled with and kept in some fancy barn. She was an odd one too, so maybe it's just the family way."

"I somehow think I met her once, maybe when I stayed that summer with Aunt Alice. Was she dark-haired?"

"Wore it swept back like a man, but on her it worked. She was very dashing. I can't recall how she died, but in her will, she left everything to the niece, who probably has enough to live on, because she doesn't do anything that anybody can see."

"Well, maybe she does something she just doesn't talk about."

"Like what?" Marney's eyes widened, probably at the thought there might be something someone didn't talk about, since she talked about everything that blew through her brain.

"I don't know."

"Well, some say she's a loner, and some say she's a hooker. Now there's something she wouldn't want to talk about! I can tell you one thing. The wives around here keep their husbands away from her. I don't let Ralph near her."

"Good idea," I said. *For her sake.* It wasn't lost on me that women will turn on other women quicker than a man will, to curry favor with men, even when the men aren't around. Maybe that's why several of my female friends sided with Ben after the divorce, or maybe I was just a lousy friend and Ben was more emotionally accessible. *Maybe I'm the loner and the hooker that Marney referenced.* I started a mental count of my failed love affairs and stopped at twelve—a dozen of anything is enough. How could none of those affairs have been even remotely satisfying?

I thanked Marney for the hospitality and made my escape, heading into town for a few items from the drugstore.

❖

Muskie Drugs had a soda fountain in back and a comic-book rack in the front. In between was every basic item a person could need for poison ivy, jock itch, hair color, or minor cuts, and things I couldn't imagine anyone needing, like a Muskie key chain, a hairnet with God Bless America on it, and a tiny crossbow that fired toothpicks in case your children felt the urge to blind one another.

A skinny schoolgirl in tight jeans and sporting a rose tattoo on her forearm rang up my toothpaste and magazines.

"So you're meeting everybody," she said. "Not hard in a town this size. Say you're from New York."

"I am." I introduced myself.

She extended her hand. "Casey Williamson," she said, and I realized the name Williamson was on the drugstore and the hardware store. "I dream about that. I've read about the subways and Fifth Avenue and all the big theater shows. I want to go to college near there so I can take the train and see it all."

"I'll bet you do every bit of that and more." I smiled at her.

"You think so? She twisted a long strand of her strawberry-blond hair.

"Absolutely." I flashed her a big smile.

"Heard you met Frank and he gave you the tour…he killed his wife, ya know?" She said it as if it were part of his name: Frank who killed his wife.

"But he didn't go to jail," I said.

"No." She paused. "Sure didn't. His wife, Dolores, used to come in here. She was a real kind lady. Frank's a badass. He tried to rape me once." She was babbling like a kid not knowing when she was over-sharing. "I was babysitting their three little dogs, and he came in and got all over me, but I was lucky because his wife came home and started screaming bloody murder, and Kay was cleaning out their boat house, and she ran up and hauled him off me, or it could have been real bad."

"I met a woman named Kay at Gus's tavern."

"That's her. We were in school together. She's a few years older than me."

"Did you report what Frank did to you?"

"To my mom. She runs the hardware store. My parents own both places. If we'd told my dad, he would have tried to kill Frank and gotten killed himself in the process, Mom said, so we kept it to ourselves."

"That's terrible." In fact, it was terrible on many levels: being attacked, having no one to report it to, having to hide it from your dad or he might get killed, and being the injured party but having to worry about everyone else's feelings except your own.

"Yeah." She sighed, seeming grateful to have gotten it off her chest.

"Who's the real pretty blond lady who was in here the other day?" I took a chance she would remember.

She pointed through the glass doors at Levade entering the hardware store across the street. "She's the coolest thing up here. I want to look that hot at her age."

I assured Casey that hot was on her horizon, as I dashed out the door and across the street, entering the hardware store where I'd bought my shotgun right over the counter. It was the largest store in town, taking up most of the block, and I told myself I wanted to look around and see what else they sold, but really I wanted to see Levade. By the time I entered, she'd disappeared into the back of the store, so I hung around the entrance, knowing she'd have to exit in that direction.

Up front was an entire area devoted to animal traps in a dozen different sizes, fishing rods and waders, snowshoes, and a case full of knives with beautifully carved handles. Little Man stood at the counter talking to Gladys, the owner, and I said hello to both of them. "Those are some powerful knives," he said, tapping the glass as if to see how sturdy it was.

"You're Casey's mom," I said to the frizzy-haired Gladys, and she said she was. "I didn't make the connection until Casey told me. A small town can be a tough place for a girl to grow up in."

She glanced at Little Man and then looked at me, as if she knew Casey had shared something personal. "Only tough in spots. Most people are real good here."

I asked to see one of the knives, so she took it out of the case, and I ran my fingers across the striated handle. The hardwood was carved in the image of a Norse forest god overlooking a wolf's head peering out of the trees. "I'm not a knife collector, but these are beautiful, and this one is very tempting, just as a piece of art."

"Knives give us strength to have what is necessary to live," Little Man said to me, then left the store as if his business there was complete.

When I looked up from the case, I saw Frank examining a bear trap. He was dressed in camo fatigues and a tight black T-shirt that accentuated his muscled biceps. I pivoted and tried to avoid him, but he'd spotted me and quickly struck up a conversation.

"I enjoyed our day together. I'd love to show you some other parts of the lake, when you have time."

"I'm actually pretty busy working on my book right now."

"Everybody needs a break." He grinned. "Can't work all the time."

Levade rounded the corner from an adjacent aisle, carrying a windbreaker. She stopped abruptly and stared at him as if she knew him and didn't like him. He spoke to me while looking directly at her, saying with undeniable pleasure, "I'm not as much a tour guide as I am a hunter, but I don't want anything to suffer, of course. Like to stalk things, pretty things, as you can tell from my collection." He glanced over at me. "But I can always postpone hunting to show an attractive lady the lake."

"She doesn't want to see the lake or anything else with you, Frank." Levade's voice was calm, but her tone was a warning.

His eyes moved to her. "We'll catch up later. Have a good one." Then he left.

Levade was visibly upset. She left the windbreaker on the counter, saying, "I'll pick this up later, Gladys," and disappeared as quickly as Frank had, ignoring me as if I weren't there.

"What was that all about?" I asked Gladys, who'd witnessed the exchange.

She shrugged like she knew the answer but wasn't sharing. Finally, she lowered her voice to a whisper. "She comes into town to shop, but she pretty much stays to herself, doesn't hang around to chat. I don't care what they say about her since she's helped out an awful lot of women here…a few men too. She knows things."

"What kind of things?"

The bell over the front door made a tinkling sound, signaling another customer had entered, and Gladys said loudly, "If you decide you want one of those knives, you let me know."

Chapter Nine

At midnight, I looked out at the lake, and there she was, the Lake Goddess, riding the white horse circling in front of the cabin, but she didn't come ashore. "She's looking at something or looking *for* something. What is it?" I asked out loud. "Levade is going to have to tell me what the hell she's doing."

Early the next morning, I walked to the Point through the woods. Not hard, I thought. I just need to keep the lake on my right in eyesight. Farther into the dense part of the forest, I momentarily lost my bearings. I reached a fork but could no longer see the lake and didn't know which direction to take, so I headed for what I thought would be the shore as a cool wind picked up. A tall woman with European features, in jodhpurs and riding boots, intersected my path, startling me.

"If you're looking for the point, it's that way," she said.

"You were on the plane! Angelique." I was so happy to see her.

"I fly occasionally."

"I'm sorry, but I thought everyone said you were no longer alive." I glanced in the direction she'd indicated, and when I looked back, Angelique was gone. I was stunned, and the hair on my neck stood up. *That's way too creepy!*

I headed in the direction she'd indicated, ending up in front of a long, rambling cabin with a nearly opaque screen, muting the glow of a long strand of tiny lights, making the place look more like a waterfront restaurant than someone's home. The water's edge was directly behind me and across from the porch steps.

Levade lay stretched out on an old slat swing, anchored to the ceiling by silver chains. She rocked above the worn and weathered porch boards and didn't get up, but spoke through the screen.

"The writer from New York who has writer's block." She seemed to enjoy saying it, mocking the small town's way of labeling people.

"What if I don't have writer's block but simply don't have anything more to say?"

She poked fun. "Spoken like a Buddha."

The two dogs were at attention, looking at me as if I were a squirrel they might need to decapitate.

"I assume the dogs are safe?"

"Why would you assume that?" She grinned.

I made no further attempt to approach them. "If I'm the Buddha, although that does seem to throw shade on my belly fat, then you're the lady of White Horse Point, whose horse avoids roads."

She stood suddenly and opened the screen door. "I've known for a while you were coming."

I have no idea what that means, I thought. Coming over to see her, coming to this town, coming into her life?

Her tone switched to flat and business-like, as if to warn me away. "You would change everything, and I don't see how that's possible now."

Despite her tone and the words she was saying, I felt like she wanted me to talk to her but was fighting the urge. She liked me but didn't want to, was even angry with herself for liking me.

"What do you mean that I would 'change everything'?"

"We'll both know soon enough," she replied, and I didn't know what to say about that, so I stuck with what I did know.

"In the hardware store, you answered Frank on my behalf. Why?"

"Because I know him and you don't."

Nothing to argue about there. "I'm just curious because you silently paddle in front of my cabin—"

"I can quit doing it," she said with a grin, as if it didn't matter to her one way or the other.

This wasn't going well. "Why do you do it? I mean, late at night in the lake instead of daylight on the road?"

"Too many cars on the road. Alizar isn't fond of cars. And I can see your parking area under the pines from there. And no one on the road can see me."

"I see." My mind registered that she must be an eccentric. Nonetheless, I wasn't too happy about the cold reception. After all, she showed up at my cabin, and we'd spoken, even laughed together, and I'd treated her with respect, so why was she being so haughty? "I suppose you're sort of the self-assigned lake patrol and security detail. Well, then, thanks for caring, but I think I'm safe. Nice chatting. See you on your next lap…from a distance, of course."

I turned to head back into the woods, sorry I'd given the woman that much of me. She is mercurial and rude…and sexy, I thought. Probably her aloofness makes her sexy. Or the way she carries herself in that straight, stately posture, as if she's the fucking queen of the pines. As if on cue, the pine needles overhead brushed up against one another in the wind and, like an ethereal broom, literally swept me back around.

"I've met your aunt, at least I think it was your aunt—twice." I had no idea why I said that. In fact I felt like Angelique was whispering in my ear and making me speak.

"She told me."

"So your aunt's still alive."

"No…and yes."

I paused to take that contradiction in. I believed in ghosts in the abstract, but ghosts who insert themselves into your life were, if not unbelievable, at least chilling. Nonetheless, I'd talked to some woman named Angelique who looked absolutely real. "She told you she met me? What did she tell you about me?"

"She likes you, but of course she's operating from a different plane."

"Well, you should listen to your aunt. I think she's a pretty damned good judge of character." I spotted the tarot card symbol tacked to her porch post. "You do readings?" I don't know why I asked a woman who didn't seem to want me around to do a reading for me. *She could fuck it up just to torture me. Tell me I'll be dead in three weeks or that I'll lose my mind and remarry Ben.*

"Would you like me to read for you?"

"I didn't bring my wallet. Maybe next time." *My chance to escape.*

"My 'welcome to the woods' gift."

She joined me on the wide porch steps, signaled the dogs, and they ignored me, going back to sleep under the porch swing. From a black velvet bag, she extracted a deck of worn tarot cards. "Concentrate on what you want to know, relax your mind, and draw several cards." I was fixated on her long, slender legs and perfect breasts, and on the light on her features that turned her from woman to man, and girl to woman.

I did as she asked, thinking at this very moment, I would like to know if I will ever find someone I truly love. I don't know where that thought came from. Only last week I'd made a pact with myself to trade true love for fame and fortune.

She touched the cards and stared at them for several minutes. Then she took my hand, turned it skyward, and brushed her fingers across my palm, and the wind trailed after her touch. My skin tingled all the way up my arm and onto my neck, my blood pressure skyrocketed, and I thought I'd pass out. She looked at my palm carefully, slowly drawing her index finger down every line in my hand.

"You've never really known love. You are in constant conflict with men. You've been waiting…for something or someone. It's in front of you now…right here." She pointed to a card with a queen on it. "But danger is associated with it. Some risk. That's all I see."

"What kind of danger," although I didn't care what kind. I just wanted her to keep holding my hand. *Why do I want this strange woman to keep touching me?*

"Your voice has been hiding in your work. It's public yet silent. Until you 'say it,' you can't 'have it.'" She dropped my hand, got up, took her cards and went back onto the porch, then disappeared into the darkened house.

Well, that was a rude good-bye. I sat for a moment mulling over her mysterious words. *What am I not saying?* Then I walked into the woods. I could make out a muted image of a car slowly passing by on the road behind her cabin, and I stopped. Maybe she's in danger herself. Maybe I just don't like the idea that she has other friends. I'm not her friend. I don't even know her.

The car disappeared down the road, but I stayed and watched as she came back out onto the porch, opened the black velvet pouch again, and extracted the worn cards, which she laid out on the table. Drawing three, she stared at them and finally shook her head from side to side as if telling herself no, then said something that sounded like "too dangerous."

Chapter Ten

S aturday night, I heard a soft but somewhat formal knock at my door. Not the kind of knock that says, "Hey, it's your neighbor," but a more tentative, respectful knock, and on the lakeside, where no one ever entered. I opened the door and there she was. My heart skipped over several times, and I just stood there smiling at her.

"Would you like to have dinner with me on the island?" she asked, seeming far more normal than when we'd last met.

"Now?"

"Yes."

"Do I need to bring anything?"

She shook her head no.

I was in shorts and a T-shirt and tennis shoes, but I didn't dare request time to change, for fear she might go up in a puff of smoke since she was so mercurial. I locked the door and followed her over the embankment and down to the shoreline, this time not landing on my behind. She laughed anyway.

"Are you remembering that I fell down this hill the last time we met?"

"I remember that my aunt said I would recognize you because you would fall."

"Angelique said I was clumsy?" That revelation put me off a little.

"She said that's how I would recognize you. She made no comment as to your agility."

I liked the rather elegant way she phrased things, carefully choosing her words. And I liked the way she moved—strong strides and then leaps like a dancer.

"How do we get to the island?"

"I have a boat." She shot me a look. *And she never forgets anything*.

I climbed into her duck boat—a wide, flat-bottomed, green metal craft that was sturdy but slow—and she motored off out of the cove, handling the boat as someone would who's done it all her life.

All around the lake were neat boat docks with small fishing craft tied to them, belonging to a tiny armada of fishermen here for a few weeks of recreation. About a mile farther, into the middle of the lake, a small island rose out of the water. Guiding the boat onto the shore, she told me to step onto the land, not into the water, because there was no beach. I stepped onto the boat's first metal bench seat, then bounced off it to the second, and then leapt onto the prow and made another leap onto land, trying to appear agile, in case Angelique is watching, I thought, but truthfully, in case Levade is watching.

The underbrush was heavy, the island uninhabited save for a few rain-soaked campfires left behind, a sign that others had enjoyed this reclusive spot.

She spread an old horse blanket, bearing the initials LF discreetly stitched in one corner, onto the ground and unpacked our dinner from a modest tan wicker basket, which gave me a few minutes to look at her. She was small, but her short-sleeved T-shirt revealed tan and sculpted arms, and the calves of her legs were muscled. She was physically quick, but wary of her surroundings like a small animal. Her hair was more than blond. It was golden, and it seemed to swirl in directions that focused you on her ethereal blue eyes. Her ears were small and close to her head, and her nose aristocratic, like those I'd seen on Grecian marble busts. She had a relatively long neck that led to a determined chin and a magnificent smile, which she flashed in my direction as she unpacked chicken and some sort of pasta.

"I thought you'd be vegan," I said.

"I thought you'd be fried chicken." She smiled and then gave me a penetrating stare that didn't feel like we were talking about fried chicken. I swallowed nervously. *Why does this woman make me so uncomfortably excited?*

She asked if I liked the food, and I told her it was the best fried chicken I'd ever eaten, and it was, but I wasn't hungry. My stomach was in knots, over what I had no idea. I was just nervous and jittery and happy. It was as if she had an energy field around her, and I had entered it and started vibrating to a frequency I'd never known.

I smiled at her, and she said, "You know of course that you have a very sexy smile. You should never stop smiling."

"Not a hard request in this environment," I said, and never stopped smiling. "How did you end up here?"

"I invited you to dinner." She grinned mischievously and then grew serious. "I came to stay with my aunt Angelique when I was young, to help with the horses. When she died, she left the cabin and land to me. And before you ask, I promised her I wouldn't sell it. I was raised forty-five minutes from here. My parents divorced a long time ago, and my mother died of dementia six months ago. So it's me, and Alizar, and of course Angelique."

"Doesn't make for a very big Thanksgiving dinner," I said. "My parents live on a small farm in Missouri, and I don't see much of them. Ben, my ex, didn't like the center of the country. But it's on me. I could have taken a vacation and gone there if I'd wanted to."

"Why didn't you?"

I laughed. "You're the psychic. You tell me."

She pursed her lips and was silent for a moment, then drew little symbols in the dirt with one finger as she spoke. "They don't like what you write…too many murders. And they wish you'd married a nice farm boy twenty years ago and given them grandchildren."

"You *are* psychic."

"You should go see them." She brushed away her drawings with the palm of her hand.

"Is something wrong? Are they sick?"

"No. You just need the connection."

"I'll put that on my to-do list. That's quite a subzero promise you made your aunt, that you'd never leave here. Don't you get lonely, particularly when summer is over?"

"Sometimes. But my aunt promised me…" her tone indicated even she knew the promise was a bit futile, "that if I would stay, she would send me someone who would love and protect me."

"And has she made good on her promise?"

"Over the years, she's sent me a few people." Her eyes were suddenly riveted on me. "But she and I have different taste in women."

My heart slapped against my chest as it had in the subway when I thought a woman's life was in danger, perhaps this time mine.

"I've talked to her about that." She laughed, and I found myself giddy and laughing along with her.

So I'm on an island with a gorgeous lesbian, or bisexual, or pan-sexual who has prepared me a picnic dinner, and I don't want to delve into the meaning of that, and I don't want this evening to end.

"I think I was behind you one day when you were in the post office." I nervously changed the subject as we ate. "You don't talk very much when you go into town."

"You followed me."

My cheeks flushed. "I did. Because there's no one up here who—"

"Because you like the way I look." Her pointed delivery skewered me whenever I tried to state something that wasn't perfectly true.

I must have gone from red to purple, because she laughed. "There's nothing wrong with liking the way people look. I like the way you look. You have an elegant but just slightly disheveled appearance. Like you know how to dress but you don't really care. My aunt was like that, and she was more psychic than I am, but she didn't advertise it. Why are you here, Taylor?" Her tone startled me. I felt like I'd been voted off the lesbian love-island and deposited on a therapist's couch. "It's not just about writing."

"Well, good question," I said, giving myself time to decide what I wanted to share. "I've been married, and, in fact, I've had several other relationships, but nothing's really worked. Men are so different from women."

"How's that?"

"Men are 'in the moment'—let's eat, let's fight, let's fuck. Women are more in their heads—let's think about it, analyze it, organize it. So when you put men and women together in a relationship, they're just not seeing things the same way, or maybe I'm not your normal woman. Anyway, emotional connection with my lovers was always my challenge, so I'm told, and it got worse with Ben. I've been jammed, and that's affected my ability to write, and, I guess, I've been trying to...waiting to..." I paused, searching for the right words.

"To feel something." Levade supplied them.

"Yes." I hadn't really been able to articulate that idea, and it seemed to beg that I reveal more than I wanted to, so I quickly shifted to a lighter topic. "Feeling something is easier in the city, because you're always in sensory overload, but I'm not a true New Yorker. Having been raised in Missouri, I struggle a bit with the culture—lusting after Gold Rush nail polish at a hundred and thirty thousand dollars a bottle, or craving a massage from a Japanese guy who jumps up on the massage table and walks on your back."

"You don't like massages?"

"I do. It's just not something..." And before I could finish the sentence, she was behind me, rubbing my neck and shoulders. Her hands, intensely strong, massaged up and down my arms, then clasped my neck, kneading the tightness, running up and down my spine, massaging each vertebrae, her palms coming to rest beside one another at the nape of my neck, then separating quickly, whereupon she grabbed my shoulders, squeezed firmly, and then threw her hands into the air as if discarding my pain into the universe.

"Your energy is blocked," she said, and I moaned, though I could just as easily have toppled over or gone into a trance. I felt like I was up above the pine trees, over the lake, floating with a feeling so warm and relaxing I never wanted her to stop. "You're way too tense," she added for good measure, and then suddenly, I felt her focus shift.

Before I could thank her for the amazing massage, she had danced away and was packing up the basket and folding the blanket, as she signaled for my silence. I was physically limp and completely confused as she hurried us into the boat.

A silver flash of light from the metal prow of a fishing boat caught my eye, and I could barely make out two men mooring their craft on the opposite side of the island.

"Who are they?" I whispered.

"People I don't want to see."

I caught a glimpse of them. "I think that's the taxidermy guy, Frank, but that's not his boat."

Levade didn't answer but deftly rowed us away from the island, apparently not wanting the motor to give us away. The oar clamps rubbed against the oarlocks, making a rhythmic metallic squeak with each stroke, and I wondered if the men on the island heard it in the quiet of the evening.

"Did he really kill his wife?" I whispered.

"Yes," she said, and put more force behind her rowing.

She pulled in at my dock and I hopped out.

"Aside from escaping pirates and fleeing the island, this has been the best evening I've had in a long time. It was wonderful. Would you like to come up to the cabin?"

"I better not." She seemed to be warring with herself on that decision. "You're an addictive woman. Must be the smile," she said, and pushed back, motoring off to the Point. I watched her until she disappeared.

Addictive. I smiled to no one.

Opening my computer, I typed in Levade, and a definition popped up describing a movement made in the show ring during which a horse raises its front legs, tucks his back legs under him, and balances on his deeply bent back legs, forelegs drawn tight.

I looked at the dictionary photo of a beautiful white horse performing that movement. It takes such balance to keep from falling, I thought, and wondered if the same was true for Levade.

That night I couldn't stop thinking about her. She was in the moon and the reflection on the lake. She was in the whisper of the pine needles. Why was I feeling this way? *Because she's psychic, and she's opened my third eye, or cleansed my aura, or elevated my kundalini, or some damned thing.* I tried to push the feelings back, but all I wanted was to see her again...alone.

Chapter Eleven

For the first time in a long time, I spent my entire day writing. The phone rang, but I ignored it. In between writing and brewing coffee, I walked over to the picture windows and glanced at the Point to see if Levade was there. No sign.

The book was taking shape. The ex-wife was going to find love, perhaps with the most unlikely man she'd ever met—an artist whose sensuality drew her to him, even as her mind was telling her he wasn't man enough, he wasn't her type, he wasn't any of the things she thought she wanted, until he kissed her.

That night, excited by the return of my creativity, I walked through the woods hoping she was home. I was wearing my one nice pair of slacks and a pale-green sweater, and carrying a bottle of wine from the only place in town that sold wine, Gus's tavern. I'd summoned the courage to go back to the tavern and buy a bottle, owning my outburst and apologizing to Gus but quickly adding, "No making fun of women behind their backs."

We shook hands and he said, "By jiminy, you're almost as tough as Levade!" So in spite of pretending he didn't know her name, he did, and privately he respected her. How did that come about?

As I approached her cabin, a voice in me said this must be how gay women date, but I quickly rejected that voice, reminding myself that I was a straight woman. But then I nearly forgot that fact when Levade opened the door, looking spectacularly beautiful in shorts that showed her tanned legs. Even better, she seemed happy to see me.

"Well, look at you!" She scanned me with those gorgeous blue eyes. "Are we having an evening?"

"That was my plan," I said, and she stepped back, inviting me in.

Her home was shack-chic. Birds' nests and paddles, fishing nets and wildlife carvings, and horse photographs everywhere, yet the entire place was neatly organized like a master's class in cabin Kondo.

In several photos a woman was riding or working horses. "Is this you?" I asked, and she nodded. "So you're a talented horse trainer like your aunt. Did you train Alizar?" She has beautiful, graceful hands, I thought.

"Do you think horses take a rider bareback out into a dark lake at midnight without a little training?"

Always the arch reply, as if she knows something I don't know. I'll bet it's an attitude that's kept a lot of people away from her.

"Why don't people in town know what you do?"

"Because they wouldn't appreciate it. They'd ask me to bring my horse over for their child's birthday party."

"But what if they're saying disparaging things about you because they don't know you?"

"What's your point?"

"None." I laughed at her elegant sense of self. She would not be diminished.

"Before it's too dark, could I meet Alizar?"

"Of course." She leaned out the back door, and just the sound of the squeaking screen brought the horse running. He paused on seeing me, sniffed, pawed, and then ambled over, deigning to allow me to touch him.

"He's so lovely!" I said, thinking she was so lovely. "What do you do with him at night, when he's alone out there and bears are around?"

She took me by the arm and guided me to an attached building right up against the back of the cabin. "Don't trip over the hose. That's how I wash the lake water off him after a swim." Her grasp felt so natural, as if she should always have my arm and I should always be with her. "Here's his little barn," she said. "I moved him out of the larger barn and built this one. I put him in at dark and close his window. He's safe. And if there's any sound of trouble, my bedroom is right up against his wall. He's a beautiful and communicative soul," she said, rubbing his head. "He knows things."

"That's what people say about you," I replied.

"That makes me a good partner for Alizar. Partners have to be able to communicate at every level." She raised an eyebrow in my direction as if hinting I might practice that suggestion. "He and I do that. I know how horses think. They've spent centuries at the hands of men who hurt them, in order to try to make them bend to their will, by breaking their spirit. But like women, the horse is smarter, and patient, and mystical, and the horse will survive."

"Alizar is a lucky horse," I said, and I meant it. *He gets to put his muzzle in her beautiful neck and breathe in that cologne she wears. What in the world am I thinking?*

"Lucky me," she said, and we moved back indoors.

She went to the fridge and pulled out a block of cheese, deftly cut several wedges on a small wooden cutting board, placed a few crackers alongside, and set it on a low birch-wood table in the living room along with glasses for the wine. Everything she did spoke of casual elegance, as if she'd been raised to operate and think differently.

I opened the bottle and poured the wine and, after a few sips, noticed she barely drank, and was probably doing it just to be polite. I was drinking to calm my erratic heart rate.

"I find you...your life...very intriguing."

"Why is that?" Her voice was sensually smooth, and although I knew she was younger, she somehow felt wiser than I was. Or maybe she just has her act together and I don't, I thought, and then I conducted a little self-therapy. I am doing just fine, actually.

"For starters, the way you spent time with your aunt and her horses. That's a great beginning for a girl."

"It wasn't all that romantic. My mother and stepfather argued. My mother sent me to be with my aunt, probably to protect me, but at the time I didn't understand that, and I was angry because I thought I'd been rejected. My aunt was tall and strong, and she became my role model. I copied the way she dressed, and what she did with horses, and even her name, Bisset, my mother's maiden name. Of course my aunt was nearly six feet tall, so someone my height couldn't look exactly like her." She laughed lightly and quickly turned the conversation to me, asking about my marriage.

"I married because friends said if I waited much longer, no one would be left but married men and gay guys. I married at thirty-three and divorced Ben when I turned forty-three, four years ago." She can do the math, I thought. "I liked Ben's sense of humor, but I didn't love him, and he was bad in bed, or I was, one or the other. Let's just say we weren't a match. In addition, he was controlling and accusing, and I let him do it because it wasn't worth the fight. That's so odd, because I have a lot of fight in me, but I didn't use it on Ben." For the first time I stopped to think about my lack of fortitude as we sipped our wine in silence.

"So everything you experienced wasn't 'for nothing,' the way you think," she said. "It helped you create, and it helped create you."

"I haven't been creating much lately." I appreciated her comforting me, but I didn't want to get into my life with Ben. In fact, I felt she could use some comforting herself. Finally, after an hour, I was relaxed enough to tell her so.

"I'll bet it's difficult just to have an ordinary friendship with someone because everyone wants you to read their cards or tell them what their future will be. I want you to know you don't have to do that with me. I don't need that from you."

"What do you need from me?"

Her directness unnerved me. She had this manner of relaxed chatting, and then, boom! It was like sticking your hand in an electrical socket. My heart jammed in my chest, and my breathing seemed to stop.

"I've been asking myself that," I murmured, as my body inclined toward hers, and my brain completely shut down, leaving everything up to my heart. I wanted more than anything to kiss her. For a split second I was sure she wanted that too. *What am I doing?* The physical sensation was so overpowering that it short-circuited my rational mind. I was no longer thinking, just feeling.

"You probably know what I need more than I do." My lips were close to hers, but she made no effort to close the gap. She merely ducked her head, and I could no longer see her face. I felt she'd willed a wall between us.

I paused and then blamed my behavior on the chardonnay, saying, "But right now, I'm thinking I've had sufficient wine, and I need to go home."

She stood up. "I'll walk with you."

Her offer to escort me back to my cabin clearly communicated she didn't share my feelings. I took a beat. "I know the way back. It was a nice evening, and thanks for hosting me uninvited."

She said nothing but watched me go.

On the way through the woods, I thought about what had happened. Maybe she thinks forty-seven is too old for her, or I'm not her type. Or she doesn't like the way I look—too disheveled, although she said she liked that. Or I'm too non-equestrian for her—she did make that remark about me being fried chicken. And what in hell am I doing coming on to some woman in the woods! I show up uninvited and hit on her. I think I've truly lost my mind! I'm not into women to start with. Men may be bad in bed, but they're obviously less complicated.

This is soooo life, I said to myself. A great thing happens, like my desire to write and create returns, and on the same day a bad thing happens, like I'm rejected by a…a…great-looking woman. It's just to keep me balanced. The universe doesn't want me toooo happy. But you would think the universe could give it twenty-four hours between good and bad. I don't think that's asking too fucking much! And I fell into bed and drifted right off to sleep.

Chapter Twelve

It had been almost three weeks since I arrived on the lake, when Judith, a woman in her early fifties, and her elderly mother, retired Judge Robertson, checked into the red cabin. Marney introduced us, dragging me to their doorstep. I didn't want to go.

"Of course you have to meet them, so you don't shoot them! I heard you bought a gun and that Sam gave you lessons. That Sam is one handsome fellow." Marney eyed me, clearly waiting for me to confirm that Sam was indeed handsome, but I refused to fuel her obvious matchmaking desires.

Marney banged on the screen door, and a tall, dark-haired woman appeared, looking like Joan Collins in *Dynasty*, if Joan had taught law at the university in Minneapolis. She was slightly taller than I was, perhaps five foot nine, but wearing spike heels, which made her look both dramatic and imposing, if not a bit overdressed for the woods.

"Well, hello, Taylor James. I recognize you from your book-jacket photo," the woman said, letting me know immediately that she'd read my work. "I'm Judith Robertson." She extended her hand, revealing long, tapered fingers ending in bright nail polish and a retro ID bracelet, which made me think she feared getting lost in the woods and needed to tag herself. "Come in!"

Marney was atwitter and marched into the living room as if leading a parade. "This is Judge Robertson." She presented the woman in the wheelchair with a flourish normally reserved for the royal family. Judge Robertson was dark-haired and dressed in a conservative black suit jacket and slacks, and she had the air of someone who knows how smart she is. She was cordial, but even less excited than I was about me popping into her living room for a spontaneous chat.

"Taylor's here this summer because of her writer's block, but she's working that out," Marney said happily.

"Oh?" Judge Robertson seemed startled by the personal-reveal only seconds after my arrival, and I couldn't help but chuckle.

"'Oh?' Indeed," I said. "You'll soon learn that everyone up here gets a descriptor. I'm 'the author with writer's block.'"

"So I'll be the woman in the wheelchair?"

"If you're lucky." I was joking. "It could be something worse." She laughed, and I liked her more than her daughter. We made small talk, but I never took a seat, saying I'd let them settle in. Judith followed us to the door.

"It's so nice to meet you. My mother really liked you. I hope you'll find time to chat." Her tone begged an invitation for coffee and conversation, but I was focused on the book and, in truth, on Levade, the only person I wanted to talk to.

"Your mother is charming," I said, ignoring the request for a chat. Marney bubbled over as I sprinted toward my cabin. "Now that was so nice. You and Judith probably know some of the same people."

Marney's upbeat attitude seemed to bring out the worst in me. I wanted to say, "Marney, Judith is a law professor in Minneapolis. I am a writer in New York. Who are these 'same people' we would know?' But instead I said, "Thanks for the introduction. I've got to get back to work."

❖

For the next four days, I stayed at the cabin and worked and fretted over what had happened, or not happened, with Levade on the Point. Anger and anxiety fueled my writing, and my fingers flew across the keys describing how this artist, whom the heroine thought she loved and who was so erotic and sensual that a mere kiss owned her, had now proved to be nothing more than an artistic version of all the other men she'd known.

❖

By Thursday, I set the manuscript aside, acknowledging that I was out of almost anything to eat and had to go to Muskie Market for groceries.

Helen whooped on my entering the store as if I'd just portaged a canoe across the Canadian border and made it back alive.

"Wonderin' if you was just eatin' skunks and badgers." She laughed. "Haven't seen ya in a week!"

I explained I was writing and could go days without looking up, but hunger had finally changed that. She said she'd saved a few things for me. "Thinkin' ya might want some fresh raspberries, like you got last time, and some local honey." I expressed my gratitude.

"You never save us any special berries or nothin' like that," a big gal in her late thirties joshed, and I was fixated on her midsection, which resembled a series of inner tubes wrapped in bright-red spandex.

"I'm feeling left out." Her friend, a shorter version of spandex-lady, chimed in with more teasing, until Helen finally flapped her hand at them, as if to say they were just "carrying on."

"Hey, raspberry girl." The big woman pointed at me as if I were standing in a lineup. "I'm Leona and this is my runnin' buddy Marilyn. Heard you're out on the lake. Wondered if you'd like to join a bunch of us gals and go bear-baiting?"

"Is that a thing?" I asked.

"Is it a thing? Yeah, it's a big damn thing…in the garbage pits on the backside of the dump."

"Do the bears die?"

"Do the bears *die*?" She snorted at my ignorance. "No, the bears don't die! We haven't even lost any people, although you could be the first. You just toss raw meat into the pit, and the bears come, and you get to see them up close, cuz they're not paying attention to you."

"Okay. I'll meet you, and follow you in my car." I spoke without thinking.

"She doesn't want to ride with us, Marilyn. Uff-da!" Leona expressed colloquial distaste.

Helen came back up to the counter. "The woman has common sense. No one wants to ride with you!"

"Nine o'clock tonight right here, and we'll head out." Leona jabbed my chest with her finger, and I felt like a butterfly being pinned to a specimen board.

I don't know why I accepted such a bizarre invitation from two total strangers. But my sexual energy was back up, making me restless and nervous, and bear-baiting sounded so horrible and at the same time a once-in-a-lifetime experience, something to regale people with in New York. Besides, Helen knew them, so it wasn't like my voyage with Frank.

❖

Leona and Marilyn were drunk when they screeched to a stop in front of the Muskie Market at nine p.m. I'd donned a pair of jeans and a sweatshirt, and wished Helen was working late so she'd be a witness to me leaving with them, in case I didn't return. I waved to the duo out of my car window and tried to keep up as they careened down the highway, then took a sharp turn onto a gravel road that quickly became dirt. The dump was up ahead, ten miles north of town on another chain of lakes called Hammertoe.

The signs as we neared the dump designated this the official TOWN OF MUSKIE DUMP SITE, and a huge iron gate marked the entrance. A vertical plank protruded from the ground with the dump hours painted on it, but no sign of animals or people. Aside from the big gates, there was no fence, so anyone could walk around the gate rather than go through it. Kind of like cabin locks, the gate didn't seem serious. They might as well have posted a sign that said, PLEASE DON'T WALK AROUND THIS GATE, instead of the sign that said, STAY OUT. *Perfect place to dump people you never want to hear from again.*

Leona's tires ripped around the closed iron gates, and across the dump and around the north side, to a humongous hole in the ground with about fifteen cars parked atop it, their lights shining across the rim of a deep pit. Several of the men had battery-powered searchlights that beamed down into the darkest crevices of the crater.

Everyone had a bottle of beer in hand, and a few of the men had their vehicles backed up to the edge of the cavernous hole, their trunks open and lined with blood-pooling plastic, making it easier to sling ten-pound pieces of raw meat out of the back and into the pit without trashing their car or truck bed. I glanced into a trunk at the pile of remains. *Must be what a mobster's car looks like when he's trying to dispose of the body.*

Meat flew through the air and landed down below, where the lumbering black bears shambled back and forth picking it up and devouring it. It seemed disrespectful to the bears, turning them into a bad circus act. It was, nonetheless, mesmerizing in its otherworldliness. I didn't feel comfortable and kept having dark thoughts. Maybe just like the subway pusher, some crazy, beer-guzzling guy would shove someone over the side, into this grand canyon of carnivores.

"Idn't this the wildest thing you ever seen?" Leona asked me, arching her back against the hood of her car as she slugged down a beer, revealing a large expanse of bare belly with tattooed flowers that rode her waves of flesh and disappeared into a large hole, euphemistically known as her navel, where a brass belly-ring protruded. Her arched position seemed to be more of a topographical advertisement than the most effective way to drink beer.

"Well, lookee who's here." Marilyn swooned as Frank Tinnerson ambled over, and I realized who her advertising was targeting. He gave her a hug and leaned over and kissed the top of her huge breasts, which were struggling to escape her NIPPLE NATION T-shirt, flashing those blue eyes up at her. He was dressed all in black—hunting boots, jeans, shirt, bandana, and an ornate MUSKIE CHAMPION belt buckle, featuring a man swinging an enormous fish over his head.

"How are my girls?" he shouted, then focused on me. "Now what are you doing running with these two, who'll get you into nothing but trouble, I promise you." They laughed, and I was pretty sure Frank's being here wasn't coincidental. "You're in for a treat. Lemmee show you somethin'." He put his arm around my waist and dragged me ten feet away to the edge of the pit. "See that mama bear right there?" He pressed on my upper back, forcing me forward to peer over the edge. "She's meaner than any of these boy bears ever thought of being. She'd bite yer head off as soon as look at you. And don't be fooled. If they ran out of meat down there, next stop is us. Can I get you a bear...I mean a beer?" And he laughed at his joke.

We walked toward the beer coolers, past two cars with the radio blaring and bare butts in the air, boffing in the backseat. The groans and shouts and car-rocking didn't turn anyone's head but mine.

Leona and Marilyn, apparently having done their job, had moved on, leaving me with Frank. I hadn't been there thirty minutes, but I could sense trouble brewing. Something about Frank made me feel trapped, like a seat belt that wouldn't unbuckle. I'd now seen bear-baiting, and I was done with it.

My mind raced as I thought about how to leave, suspecting Frank would try to stop me. I did have one party trick that had gotten me out of trouble before. I could throw up on cue—or at least sound like I was going to.

As Frank kept cuddling me, and pulling me along with him, I went into full-boat stomach-virus vomiting noises. One thing about men, they usually run from a woman vomiting, bleeding, or giving birth, so Frank backed away. I walked backward toward my car, still gagging, and a throng of beer-bellied bear-baiters parted like the Red Sea. "So sorry, I'm terribly sick," I said, and got in my car and locked the doors, thinking, actually I was telling the truth. Massive chunks of meat dripping in blood, hungry bears slurping the cow carcasses down, bare butts in the air copulating above the bears, and being cuddled by a guy who killed his wife did make me a tad queasy.

❖

Saturday night, adopting my "just friends" mode, I used my bear-baiting adventure as an excuse to stop by and see Levade. She was home and seemed glad to see me; however, I reminded myself that it often started out that way, and then later, not so much. I told her I'd had the most unusual night of my life at the bear pits.

"I went with Leona and Marilyn. Do you know them?" I asked.

"I know who they are." I gathered she was applying the "if you can't say something nice" rule.

"I've never seen so much beef being slung around—in truck beds, the bear pit, and in the backseat of cars! It was the strangest combination of raw pleasure and rancid entertainment I've ever witnessed. Frank was there, and I had to pretend I was sick to get away from him."

Levade wasn't viewing my adventure as humorous, and she interjected, "Promise me you'll stay away from him completely."

I paused. "Has he done anything to you, or said anything to you?"

"I know what he's capable of. Promise me." *What more, beyond the murder of his wife, could Frank be capable of?*

"I want nothing to do with him. He's the reason I bought a gun. I didn't know he'd be at the bear pits. His appearing was less coincidental and more like an ambush." After a long pause, I finally said, "Well, just had to share my extracurricular activities. I'll head back to the cabin."

"I'd like it if you would stay."

My heart leapt. *She is actually inviting me to spend more time with her.*

"Only if you tell me about your life and loves," I joked, thrilled by the invitation.

"Does everything have to be a story for you?" she teased.

"Yes, of course. So please make it interesting." I gave her my "addictive" smile.

"Let's see." Her tone showed she was toying with me. "In my youth I was living with my aunt, who was painfully afflicted with lovesickness, because she was madly in love with someone who was married. I watched her, lost in desire and sadness, and told myself I would never let that happen to me. After she died, my life has been with her horses and now Alizar, the one who is left, the son of my aunt's youngest and most talented stallion. Your next question is about my lovers—I've had three."

My heart jumped at the idea of this exquisite woman giving herself to another woman and what that must feel like.

"They were all the same. Sell the horse, sell the house, move with me to the city." She gestured into the air with her lovely, artistic hands.

"Did you love any one of them enough to do that?"

"I could never love someone who asked me to cut out my heart."

"If they had stayed here with you—"

"I didn't want them to stay."

We sat quietly for a while before I said, "I've had several lovers…maybe more than several. Actually, I've never been sure how many 'several' is. I wouldn't call them lovers—more like friends. I've never had a problem with friendly intimacy—sex as an exercise—because both of you know what you're getting out of it. Expectations set and met."

"So sex for you has been similar to asking someone to go jogging?" Her pretty forehead furrowed.

I laughed. "Well, I had to like them, or be very high. I don't drink that much anymore, and I don't like that many people."

"Weren't you afraid of getting an STD?" she asked in her straightforward manner.

"I was more afraid of not feeling anything. So I got married." I laughed loudly. "Oh my God, how ridiculous that sounds in hindsight! And then after ten years of *still* not feeling anything, I just tired of it. I didn't need it at all."

"It?"

"Sex, love, any of it."

"Everyone needs it. You're numb without it," she said quietly.

"Well, so I guess I've been numb...really numb."

She leaned in and took my face in her hands and slowly placed her lips on mine, and she kissed me, her mouth open and hot, her tongue in me. It was soft and sensual, the sexiest kiss I'd ever experienced, and it melted me.

"Can you feel that?" she whispered as she pulled her lips away. In response, I pulled her down on the couch and kissed her again, this time with more intensity, and parts of my body awoke that had been sleeping for decades. Her small frame curved neatly into mine, and the smell of her skin was beyond intoxicating. Heat rose in my groin.

Levade turned her head to one side and glanced at the door, and I realized she thought there was danger in being with me. "I... you have to go. It's too soon," she said, rejecting me.

"I don't know what that means, but I can promise you it's not too soon." I gasped, feeling that to abort lovemaking now could cause me to implode.

"It means I'm protecting you, Taylor. Trust me."

"From what? From you, from getting hurt, from—"

"Please just go."

I got up feeling awkward, and she backed away as if she knew that one more kiss would make it impossible to separate me from her.

Maybe she can't let anyone in. I mentally attacked her for rejecting me. There's a reason she lives all alone with no one out here in the woods. And then I quickly turned on myself. Why am I psychoanalyzing her? My ability to let anyone in, or to love anyone in return, has been abysmal. But at least I know that about myself, I mentally huffed.

I seemed unable to get my bearings, as I headed back to my cabin, and I had a serious conversation with myself. Holy, God that was terrific! It was beyond terrific, whatever the next level of terrific is. Stupendous! But where does it go? Nowhere. It can't go anywhere. Get real.

Then the wind whipped up in the pines again and spun my body around against my will, and I walked back to her cabin. *I've lost my mind when it comes to this woman.*

"I have two tickets to the church dinner," I called out. And I almost laughed out loud. *If Ramona could see me now, acting like a lakeside Lothario, pretending I care about church-dinner tickets.*

Levade cracked the door and peeked around it, and all it took was that amazing smile to make me no longer care what my behavior looked like.

"Is the church dinner fun, weird? Will they try to convert me?" I asked.

"You should go. You'll like it," she said softly.

"Will I see you there?"

"Maybe." Her eyes twinkled.

The following night was Sunday, the third week in August that everyone on the lake talked about all summer in anticipation. I attended the church dinner wearing my one pair of good slacks and my Native American shirt with the ponies on it.

Every year all the churches—Methodist, Baptist, Catholic, Unitarian, and Episcopal—held their dinners at the same three-hour interval, on the same night, so tourists and locals alike could move from one church basement to the next, testing all the homemade food created by the parishioners—Norwegian ladies who learned to cook from their grandmothers. There were women I'd never seen before, who arrived from farms and cabins outside town, and men who came from logging camps out in the woods.

The women proudly dished up their special recipes and handed plates to all of us with tickets. Wild-rice casserole was a favorite, and cookbooks featuring that dish sold out. I was awash in love for this tiny town that came together to share this night of food and friendship and include strangers like me with equal affection.

A young Native American woman intercepted me in the food line at the Unitarian supper and told me she liked my shirt and it would bring me luck. I asked her about the seeming deification of wild rice, and she said that during the harvest, Native Americans paddled into the quicksand bogs and knocked the precious rice grains off into their canoes, then brought them back to the tiny processing plant, and from there they made their way into local kitchens, and even more often to other cities and towns. It was the town's one industry, and many worked there as a second job.

The food was beyond delicious, especially the desserts, and aside from having to learn that salad meant Jello and hot dish meant casserole, I was getting along just fine. I wasn't sure if it was the setting, or the friendship, or the food, but it was a perfect night. Helen and Thor greeted me on the sidewalk in front of the Methodist church, and they seemed extra jovial.

"Hey!" Thor shouted, "You eat all that food so there's none left for me?"

"I sure ate fast when I saw you coming!" I teased back, and he roared with laughter.

Gladys and Casey were inside dishing out blueberry pie, and down the street Marney and Ralph were at the Catholic Church trying to outdo all the Unitarians, everyone warm and laughing and telling jokes like one big family.

As I walked from church to church, I searched for Levade's Jeep along every street, and I looked up expectantly every time someone entered. *Where is she? Why hasn't she shown up?* Maybe she was upset over what happened between us and doesn't want to see me. My obsessing over her was marring the experience, because the experience I wanted was with her.

At my last stop, the Episcopal Church, a voice boomed, "Taylor James!" and I felt instantly shy as heads turned to see who was shouting. Judith the law professor waved excitedly, her bobble-bracelets banging against her sizeable wrist, as she wheeled her mother, the judge, down the food line. Judith's conservative A-frame skirt and high-buttoned blouse didn't seem to match her loud outburst, but since tonight's high point was apparently buffet with mom, maybe she was creating her own excitement. "We need to get together and have some fun!" she shouted.

Like play board games with your mother? I thought, and then immediately felt so wicked I agreed out loud that we did need to get together, then hurried off to avoid that happening.

Still thinking of Levade, I prepared a platter of food, covered it, and decided to take it to her so she could share in the celebration, and in truth, so I could see her.

Happy at the idea of surprising her, I drove fifteen miles to her cabin, got out, and walked through the woods to the door. It was dark and Levade wasn't there. A note was jammed in the screen door between the screen and the wooden cross pieces. I didn't remove it but simply read: "Had to go out of town. May not be back before you leave. Hope you've been inspired."

Inspired? How arrogant! Is that what that kiss was all about, to inspire me? And why does she think I'm leaving? I was inexplicably bereft and sat down on the steps for a moment to collect my thoughts. Then I got up and reread the note.

The word inspired seemed carefully chosen, perhaps so that if a stranger read it, they wouldn't know it was a personal note, but assume it was just a note for a client. I took hope that I was right. Then I looked closer at the *L* on the word leave, and it had the same flourish as the *L* on the old postcard at the cabin. *It's some kind of message. She's saying something to me. But why the big mystery? I write mysteries. I don't want my life to be one.* Depressed, I traipsed back to my cabin.

If the young Native American woman at the church dinner was right, that my shirt would bring me luck, then I needed to know who to phone to activate it, because I sure wasn't feeling lucky. At least not lucky in love. Odd thing to think.

CHAPTER THIRTEEN

L evade had vanished. I inquired, but no one in town had a phone number. Why hadn't I gotten it? *Because Muskie Lake people don't phone each other. They take cool walks and tap on screen doors in that old-fashioned, neighborly way.* But I still should have gotten her damned phone number.

I rang Ramona, more dejected than before, which was evident by the fact that I'd phoned her, something I never did. Ramona probed until she finally got it out of me.

"You had sex with the woman on the Point? Oh, my God!"

"No, not sex. Near-sex."

"What is near-sex? Are you Bill Clinton?"

"She wants me, but then she runs."

"Excuse me, but we're talking about a woman. Do I need to remind you that you're straight? You've seen more cocks than a brood of hens." When I didn't laugh, Ramona sighed. "Okay, Taylor. Listen to me! Frank, your taxidermy guy, killed his wife because she had an affair with a woman, so Frank undoubtedly hates lesbians. Frank was never arrested because apparently the men in Muskie felt that what his wife did to poor Frank and his manhood far outweighed whatever misfortune happened to one of them.

"Levade has sense enough to know it's a small town and everyone is in everyone's shorts, so unlike you, she's probably keeping her panties on to protect your ass. Think about that. If

Frank wants to date you, what could possibly go wrong if his competition is once again a woman? That has danger written all over it."

"How do you know all this?"

"Everyone in town knows all this, except the part about you lusting after women, so stop it. Maybe you'd better come back to New York. If you want sexual experimentation, this place is crawling with lesbians who'll take you to dine at Per Se, instead of some lake-bump, chigger-bitten island."

"I'm staying until I get things sorted out."

"What things?" She seemed exasperated.

"I don't know," I said quietly, unable to explain myself lately. "I just feel this amazing attachment to her. Wanting to spend every moment with her. Is that crazy?"

"Yes," she said decisively, "unless you're considering a sex change."

I tried to formulate a response or defend my feelings, but nothing came out. After a beat, Ramona broke in. "Just write something, will you? And be careful. I don't want it published posthumously."

❖

I did what Ramona suggested because I had nothing else to do. I sat at the computer and wrote, then deleted, then wrote. The story had begun as a hard-core mystery about a man stalking his ex-wife because she was having multiple, embarrassing affairs. But I found myself incorporating more love scenes than I initially intended. In fact, I never liked writing love scenes because they felt so mechanical, and now I was gravitating toward romantic encounters.

Maybe it was my current environment, the romance of the Northwoods, or maybe it was meeting Levade. *She's the most sensual being I've ever encountered. Maybe she's my muse.* That would explain my feelings.

I typed a sentence. "She looked at her with eyes that severed her soul and left her with half of who she was." Then I stared at the sentence and quickly struck the *S* from the first word. It should be *He*. HE looked at her with eyes that severed her soul. What a Freudian typo. I pushed back from the desk as if the computer were possessed and sipped my coffee, staring at the screen. Finally, I touched the key and put the *S* back. *It's a love story about two women. It's She.*

Ramona's been touting my new male-driven mystery, and I'm working on a lesbian love story. I can't help it. The S makes it sexier. The S excites me and makes me want to write the love scenes. Maybe I should write the love scenes with She *and then just change it all to* He *when I'm done. Or maybe I should just own the fact that a woman has completely upended my sexuality.*

On my next trip to town for groceries, I spotted an orange cardboard calendar tacked to a corkboard above the frozen-food section. It was headlined MUSKIE AREA EVENTS—AUGUST, a jumble of anything happening in the region this month. *True Grit* was playing at a tiny local theater, the farmers' market was open today in Pine City, and an upcoming dressage event was scheduled in Duluth. I was surprised that something as elegant as a dressage event was posted on a grocery-store tack board, but I was happy to spot it and wondered if Levade would attend the show, since she loved horses. I jotted down the dressage dates. Then feeling antsy, with nothing to do, I decided to drive to Pine City and check out the farmers' market.

The drive was beautiful, the roads winding and tree-lined, sparkling water dotting the landscape. Pine City was a small mining town, with a population approaching four thousand. The buildings were multistoried and constructed of huge lake stones, making them seem as impenetrable as a medieval fortress. The farmers' market was held in the town square, and I purchased Iowa corn and garden tomatoes and leaf lettuce and stashed them in a cooler bag in my car. Then I spotted a coffee shop. "Oh my God," I said out loud. Not a café that serves coffee, but an actual coffee-specializing shop. I headed in that direction, ebullient.

The store was crowded, packed shoulder to shoulder with coffee aficionados who had found this singular caffeine oasis. People sat in small booths drinking and chatting. I paid for a pound of ground coffee and a cup to go, and was about to walk out the door, when I glanced over at the corner booth and was shocked to see Frank Tinnerson deeply engrossed in conversation with Levade. Frank, who was supposedly dangerous, with Levade, who had mysteriously disappeared. *Is she having an affair with him? Is she warning me to stay away because there's something more between them?* A booth near them cleared, and I quickly sat down in it, feeling like a spy in a B movie.

All I wanted to do was stare at her. Actually, no, I wanted to hold her and kiss her, as I had at her cabin. The feeling overwhelmed me, as if she'd cast a spell on me.

"I still have it," Levade said, her voice low.

"I want it." His tone was forceful, perhaps even sexual, and my heart pounded as I prayed she wasn't involved with him. "This is a dangerous game." He turned menacing. "You know I won't let go of you. Not after what you did."

"It's in someone else's hands, and if anything happens, it will happen to you next."

"I'll tell you one thing, Levade. Every law-enforcement officer in the state would give his eye teeth to be the friend and fishing buddy of Frank Tinnerson, the Muskie Champion of the world. You know what I mean? In fact, some of them already have! The one thing I don't have in my taxidermy collection is a white horse. Wouldn't that look great, right there in my front window, facing the lake?" He laughed, and slapped the table, making a startlingly loud sound, then exited the coffee shop.

I took a deep breath and slid into the seat he'd just vacated. Levade collapsed back into the booth on seeing me. "What are you doing here?" she whispered, obviously drained of energy.

"My question to you. And I have an even better question. What is Frank threatening you with?"

"You have to stay out of it, Taylor."

"You're seeing him?"

"No! Of course not."

"Then why is he so obsessed with you?"

"I have some things to do here over the next couple of days," she said, not answering my question.

"I heard him threaten Alizar. That's horrible. Let me help you. I'll do anything." I meant it, regardless of what danger it put me in.

She paused, looking into my eyes and judging my sincerity, I assumed. "Okay. Pull your car up behind mine across the street," she said. I slid out of the booth and jogged to my car, got in, and moved it two blocks, parking adjacent to hers. I was behaving like a trained seal, but I didn't care.

Her car windows were cracked, and she was parked in the shade, and when she opened the Jeep's cargo area, I saw a large pet carrier inside, containing the most humongous cat I'd ever seen.

"I need you to take him," she said.

"Take him where?" I was startled.

"With you. He was my mother's cat, and Frank has threatened to kill him and stuff him to get back at me."

"Stuff him? Oh my God! But I don't know anything about cats!"

"Here's his food and litter box." She began unloading items into my car. The cat food was in twenty-pound bags, and the litter box was the size of a small wading pool. "He can't go outside because he looks so large that someone could mistake him for a wild animal and shoot him."

"Why is he so damned *big*?" I was still fixated on his sheer size.

"He's a Maine coon cat. His name is Sasquatch."

"Sasquatch, of course."

"My mother called him Sassy."

"Okay. How do I get him out when I get him home? I mean, can I just reach in there?"

"It's a cat, Taylor. If you can't do this—"

"I can do it, of course. I want to do it. I just have to…how much does he weigh?"

"Thirty pounds."

"My God, that's two cats."

She kissed me right there on the street. Not a full sexual kiss, but a kiss that was enough that I would have agreed to take a six-pack of cats if she'd asked.

She thanked me profusely as I climbed into the car and drove off, heading back to the cabin, waving good-bye to her out of the window. Sasquatch sat on the front seat. His three-foot-long frame more than filled the cat carrier, causing masses of black and gray tabby fur, and no small amount of tabby fat, to stick out between the bars. He had a perpetual frown, large hanging jowls, and tall ears standing straight up on top of his head like two little dunce caps with fur streaming from them, making him look like the pissed-off guy at the costume party. I reached over to touch his nose reassuringly, and he let out a low growl.

"Okay. You're not the pussy I had in mind, but we have to make the best of each other. And we've got to dump the silly Sassy shit. It's not you. I'm calling you Sass." He stretched to the extent possible given his tight quarters and let out a big sigh, as if relieved by the name change.

By nightfall, Sass was out of his cage and stalking around the cabin like a mountain lion checking everything out. I closed my bedroom door, feeling vulnerable in my nightshirt to cat scratches and hoping he wouldn't claw anything in the living room. Suddenly the door began to vibrate, and then the door handle rattled violently. I could see Sass's huge paw, pad-side up, clasping the underside of the door, shaking it vehemently, clearly demanding I let him in. I told him to stop it, but that only seemed to infuriate him, making him shake the door louder.

I finally relented and opened it. His big green eyes glowed in the dark like alien orbs, scaring the hell out of me, so I pulled the quilt up to cover my face. He bounded up onto the bed and draped his entire body over my head. After extracting him twice, I gave up. "Look, I know you're upset, and you've lost your owner, and you're being dragged around to strange places, and you don't know what's to become of you, but do I really deserve this?" I tilted my head to the side to question the cat, who was snoring so loudly his upper lip was vibrating. *A thirty-pound cat sleeping on my head, all because I crave the Lake Goddess. What has become of me?*

❖

At dawn, I called Ramona to ask her what she knew about feeding a cat this size.

"I didn't get the feeding instructions from Levade, and every time I put a little food down for Sasquatch, he eats it and screams for more. At what point does a cat just bloat and die? And who would even recognize bloat in a cat this size?"

"You're keeping her cat?" Ramona fixated on his mere existence. "Does he claw anything?" She was protective of her cabin.

"No. He just sleeps on my head. I guess her mother let him do that."

"No wonder she lost her mind—a huge cat on her head night after night."

"Do you know anything about the feeding amounts for a Maine coon cat?"

"I have authors who call me about everything in the world, Taylor, but you're the only one who wants feeding instructions for her lover's cat."

"She's not my lover."

"Google 'cat feeding,' for God's sake. I have work to do," she said and hung up.

My lover's cat. My lover's cat. I tried the words out in my head to see how they sounded and how I felt about having a female lover whose cat I was babysitting.

Sasquatch let out a huge belch. "My stomach's upset too," I told him.

CHAPTER FOURTEEN

The whole Pine City encounter, with Frank threatening Levade and then me becoming custodian to Sasquatch, had completely derailed my thinking. I'd forgotten to ask Levade if she was planning to attend the horse show in Duluth, and more important, I had failed to get her phone number. So I would just have to press on with my plan.

I stopped over at Marney's cabin to ask if she'd check in on Sass and make sure he ate his dinner and had plenty of water. I was headed to Duluth to see a horse show.

"Oh, for fun!" she said, and I was reminded that Minnesotans put "Oh, for" in front of almost any word. Marney bubbled over. "I think that's the show that the woman on the Point goes to see every year. Helen says she takes her horse along, although I can't imagine a horse watching a horse show, but maybe it's an outing for both of them."

Levade will be there! My mind danced with the possibility of seeing her. I thanked Marney profusely for helping more than she knew.

Marney followed me back to my cabin to meet Sass, and I began to prepare her for the shock of seeing a cat his size. "Now he's perfectly harmless, but he's a big boy," I said, choosing my words carefully. "Why don't you sit in this rocker for your first meeting, kind of be on his level," I suggested. Then I opened the bedroom door, and Sass came flying out, rounded the enclosed porch, and raced into the living room like he was passing the one-mile marker at Churchill Downs, clearing the couch and the second rocker and landing on Marney, causing all the air to blow out of her body at both ends.

The force of Sass's landing tipped the rocker over backward, and Marney's head was on a trajectory with the hard floor when I scooped them both up like a ground ball and righted the rocker. Marney had completely disappeared behind a pile of fur, and I was certain Sass had blown my chances for a babysitter.

Before I could apologize, Marney swooned. "Oh, for cute! Don't you worry about a thing, Taylor. Little Sassafras and I will be juuust fine." It was clear Sass had found his true love.

Bonus round! I patted Sass good-bye before anything else could happen, hugged Marney, and told her I'd be back late. Then I hit the road.

Turning the radio up and the windows down, I sang along with Kelly Clarkson to *Love So Soft*, ecstatic I had a lead on Levade.

❖

The fairgrounds were packed with expensive horse trailers and rows of booths selling everything from spangled show jackets and expensive horse-themed jewelry, to German riding crops and tufted saddle pads. In and near the arenas, riders in shiny, knee-high boots led buffed and beautiful, high-priced horses around for a little exercise. I stood in line to buy a ticket for the day, picked up a program, and scanned the crowd for Levade.

It certainly wasn't the kind of casual horse show I'd imagined. The horses were well groomed and well trained, and they were competing for ribbons and rankings. I sat next to an older man, who seemed fixated on the horses exercising in the ring.

"Do you have a horse in the show?" he asked politely, keeping his eyes on the ring.

"No. I know next to nothing about dressage. Just an outing."

"This is a recognized FEI event, Fédération Équestre Internationale. Do you know the movements like the half pass, where the horse is moving forward and sideways on the diagonal, and the flying change, where they switch leads as they travel at a canter?" When I looked clueless, he pointed to a little insert in the program that described what the horses were being judged on. "It doesn't really matter if you know what the movements are. The horses' performances are just beautiful to watch." He pointed to a man warming up on the sidelines. "That's the passage, where the horse performs a powerful and suspended trot."

I scrolled down the list of riders, their entry numbers, their horse's name, and the time they would ride. Like a flashing neon sign, it jumped out, startling me. #312 LEVADE BISSET—ALIZAR 2:42 P.M., ARENA #1. I looked up at the logo-covered walls and spotted a big sign that said ARENA #2. I checked my watch; it was 2:10 p.m. I asked the man next to me for directions, then bolted out of the stands and jogged to the adjacent arena, skidding to a stop inside the giant doors.

Several riders were working their horses and preparing them to compete or just standing with them. In their helmets, and from a distance, the riders were nearly indistinguishable from one another, so if Levade was there, I couldn't find her.

I took a seat as close to the ring as I could. The announcer asked everyone to clear the arena. Then arena-drag equipment drove through, smoothing the dirt for the riders.

After fifteen minutes, dirt smoothed and track cleared, the announcer said, "First in arena one is Levade Bisset on Alizar, a twelve-year-old Lipizzaner stallion." Levade and Alizar cantered out to the center of the ring, stopped, and bent their heads to salute the judges. I wanted to applaud because she and Alizar were so beautiful together, and they hadn't even done anything yet.

Then the music began, and Levade, her body never moving, her hands quiet, seemed to be merely along for the ride as Alizar executed the half pirouette, half pass, and flying change fluidly and in rhythm to the music, as if he and Levade were dancing together. It was incredibly sensual to watch—an elegant woman and a powerful stallion making dramatic moves that landed right on the beat of the music. I knew enough to realize that Levade was giving him expert, invisible cues, and that the two of them were mentally in tune, more so than she was with people. After five minutes of sheer magic, Alizar came to a stop in front of the judges—halt and salute! It was beyond sexy, and the crowd went wild as the two of them exited the arena. *How many hours, days and years must they have trained together for this? I've reached a new low. I'm jealous of Alizar for dancing with her!*

I could see Levade in the exercise area, adjacent to the arena, watching through the arena doors as ten other horses went through their paces. None of them were as graceful and talented as she. At four thirty p.m., they announced the ribbon winners, and Levade took first place in her division. But her big win came at the end of the day, when the announcer intoned, "High Point for the show goes to rider number #312, Levade Bisset, on Alizar." The applause drowned out the remainder of his remarks. She re-entered the ring for the awards ceremony, took the lead spot, at the head of the riders, and circled the arena as people applauded. Then she stopped to accept her trophy as Alizar tucked his front leg under and bowed for the photographer to snap a photo. I was overjoyed. How amazingly talented. How beautiful. People crowded around her, and I wanted to be one of those people, but interrupting would disrupt her moment with all the other riders.

After the show, Levade led Alizar to a horse trailer that looked like a luxury liner, kissed his muzzle, patted his neck, and looked into his eyes for a long talk. She spoke at length with a man who took the halter rope and led Alizar up a ramp onto the trailer, and they drove away. The trailer was marked LF, and I wondered if Levade owned Alizar, or if she just trained and rode him for someone else, or if she'd just sold him. Her body language seemed to say she wouldn't be seeing him back at the Point, and I felt incredibly sad for her. I decided to walk over and speak to her privately and congratulate her, having finally understood why she carried herself so ramrod straight, moved so elegantly, and was so sophisticated. She had obviously been trained from childhood for this world of magnificent horses and elegant riders.

I was within earshot when a tall woman in riding gear approached, and Levade seemed delighted to see her. They hugged a too-long embrace, as far as I was concerned, and the taller woman slung her arm over Levade's shoulder and walked her toward the concession stand, saying, "We're all getting together for dinner to celebrate your big win." That was the end of my opportunity to speak to her.

I stopped at a booth and asked for a pen and a piece of paper and wrote, "Levade, you were phenomenal! Huge congratulations! Love, Taylor" I included my cell-phone number. A young boy in jeans and boots was watching me, and I said, "You see that woman over there who just won the big trophy? Would you take this note to her?" I handed him a ten-dollar bill for his effort. He headed in her direction, and I headed for my car. I hung around for half an hour in the parking area, hoping she might call, but she didn't.

I drove back to Muskie so thrilled that I'd seen Levade ride and so upset that another woman had her arm around her, *perhaps at this very minute!* I tried to remain calm and rational—being jealous was ridiculous—focusing on Levade's incredible performance. Who would ever have known that the woman with the white horse on the Point was a talented equestrian? Most of the people in Muskie had written her off as odd, which in fact she appeared to be. *But she's also much more. And who is that fucking woman who had her arm around her?*

🦋

Physical chemistry is a strange phenomenon. It's as if your body no longer belongs to you, but is owned by someone else who calls it like a siren, day and night, never letting up and keeping you in a state of euphoria and unrest, alternating with anxiety and irritability.

August was drawing to a close. Levade hadn't returned, and I couldn't stay away. I walked to the Point almost daily and was always disheartened because I saw no sign of her. Why would she be staying in Pine City? Or had she driven there from Duluth for her meeting with Frank? Should I go back and try to find her?

On this particular, sunny morning, I ran into Sheriff Sam out on the Point. He had Levade's dogs with him.

"Noticed you come over here quite a bit," he said by way of greeting and tipped his cowboy hat. I liked the fact that he was his own man and chose a cowboy hat over a Northwood's ball cap.

"It's pretty over here" was the best I could muster.

"I sometimes trailer Alizar for her, feed him his grain when she's not here, and check on him, put him in at night. If they're gone, then I kind of use that time to get things in shape. Lotta horse manure in these parts," he said, kicking pine needles out of his way unnecessarily.

"You can say that again," and I figured Sam knew I was referencing the human kind. "I bet her horse misses her when she's not here," I said, meaning I did. "And you take care of her dogs too."

"Charlie and Duke are my dogs. When she's out here, I have these two stay with her, just in case." Just in case seemed to include everything Sam feared and couldn't talk about. "Besides, I got six more at home." He laughed, and it dawned on me that Sam had an almost familial fondness for Levade that went beyond the role of caretaker.

"Lots of pretty places to walk…" He seemed to want a better answer about what I was doing there.

"None where I might get lucky and run into a beautiful white horse, but unfortunately not today." I kept my eyes on the ground like I'd found something interesting to look at. "So how did you get this assignment?"

"I've known Levade's family for forty years. When I was a young man, Angelique befriended me. That's how I knew Levade, who was just a kid herself, and everywhere we went, Angelique would make me promise that I'd take care of her. She was always into something." He laughed, obviously enjoying the memories. "Anyway, Levade knows her horse is safe if I'm keeping everything shipshape for him. There's a six-stall barn out back that her aunt used to keep her horses in, but nowadays I store the hay there, plus the tractor and some tack. Lock it all up, of course. And her aunt created a big dirt arena back there, where she worked her horses, so I keep that cleared and dragged for Levade and Alizar."

"Will Alizar be coming back here?"

"I sure hope so." He seemed surprised I would ask.

"Sam, tell me about Frank. I just can't seem to get what happened to his wife out of my mind."

"Not much to tell really. It's all just out there in the open."

"You mean that a killer roams free and everybody knows about him? I'm sure you know a lot more than that."

Sam puffed his cheeks up and then slowly let the air out, deflated like a balloon after the party. "Could have been an accident. He took her hunting, and Dolores was an animal lover. He said he went to shoot a wolf, and she shouted 'no,' and she jumped in front of the animal just as he pulled the trigger. Frank's so damned odd, it's hard to know how much is kinky and how much is killer."

"Levade seems to be afraid of him and wants me to stay away from him."

"That's not bad advice." His voice was upbeat. "Gotta get to work. See you on my next round." Sam strode off, climbed into his truck, and drove away.

"Alizar." I spoke his name into the air as if he were here. "Talk to me. Levade said you communicate. Tell me what's going on. I wouldn't tell this to anyone else, Alizar, but I miss her terribly."

A breeze blew in off the lake and shook the pine boughs overhead. The needles quivered and rustled like the voluminous taffeta skirt of a woman who couldn't quite get settled in her chair. Then a powerful gust of wind followed, blowing my hair into my eyes. Storms blew up quickly on the lake, so I decided I'd better get back home.

As I walked by the long porch, the card tucked into the screen blew off. I don't know why I chased it, but I couldn't bear to have anything she'd touched be lost. I snatched it off the ground and turned it over in my hand. On the backside, she'd written, "Late Saturday." The *L* looked like the *L* on the postcard at my cabin. I was overjoyed to know that's when she would be back. I glanced up at the sky, thanking someone, or something, for the encouragement.

❖

I was waiting on the porch when Levade returned. She jumped slightly, obviously startled to see me.

"How did you know I was coming back tonight?" She looked weary and spoke absently, as if not mentally present but preoccupied with thoughts of something else.

"I found your note."

She examined the card and the writing that said "Saturday Late," and smiled. "This side isn't my handwriting."

That registered as a strange thing to say, but all that mattered was her presence. She was back.

"I drove to Duluth and watched you perform. You were absolutely brilliant!"

"I got your note, and it meant a lot. I thought you might come over."

You could have called me, and I would have been there in a heartbeat. Why didn't you call me? "I didn't want to interrupt. I also thought I might be a little difficult to explain to your horse crowd...like the tall woman who put her arm around you and walked you to the concession stand and then took you out for dinner."

She smiled in spite of herself. "Ah, the jealous type."

"That has not been my trademark. You were spectacular! Why didn't you tell me you were competing? I had to find out about the show in the frozen-food section at Muskie Market, for God's sake," I teased.

She smiled and shrugged. "I don't really like for anyone to know where I am."

"You mean Frank. Threatening Alizar was so horrible and unthinkable. Would he really do something like that to such a beautiful animal?"

"To the animal I love…to the people I love."

"Knowing that, why would you even meet with him at the coffee shop?"

"I told you my mother died. I was in town to sort out some of her things. I ran into Frank on the street, and he said he had something important to tell me." She sounded a bit irritable.

I wanted to believe her, but I didn't. She's seeing someone, maybe the equestrian woman in Duluth, I thought. Why not? We're not "seeing" each other. In fact, this moment felt awkward, as if I'd arrived when she had other plans or something else to do.

"Is Sasquatch doing okay? Do you want me to take him?" she asked.

"No, he's fine. He's safe with me. He's actually good company." I knew it was crazy, but I felt that if I had her cat, I had a connection to her, and I didn't want to lose that connection.

After an awkward pause, she finally said, "Do you want to come in?"

Her question had an obligatory tone that seemed to say, since you won't leave, would you like to come in.

I've spent too long feeling bad about relationships, I thought. I'm not going to continue doing it. I have more pride than that. She may be a brilliant horsewoman, but I make a living in the toughest city in the world. I need to get a grip here.

"Actually, no. I just wanted to say I won't be available much. I'm sorry for the loss of my gender-compass. It's clear that I'm straight and—"

"No one's anything—straight, gay, bi, whatever." She sounded like she was schooling a child.

"Well, I know what I am."

"In another place and time, I would show you what you are," she said, and in her eyes, I saw a longing, clearly a desire, yet a sadness, and I felt she had made a decision to pull away from me. "Good night, Taylor." She spoke quietly and went inside.

That non-breathing, fuzzy-headed, weak-kneed feeling washed over me. I turned to walk home just as a car pulled into her drive.

I hate spying. Yet I stepped behind a large tree, hidden by its girth. It was Casey, the young girl from the drugstore. My mind raced. Was Levade seeing young girls? After all, Casey said she thinks Levade is hot. That very thought made me think less of myself. *This kind of insane behavior is exactly why I need to move along, get completely away from this woman.*

Skinny and nervous, Casey walked onto the porch steps, looking back over her shoulder as if demons were following her. She sat down at a small table, and Levade joined her, their heads inclined toward one another as if they were having a secret conversation. Levade lit three candles, and the glow cast an eerie shadow over their faces. After several minutes, Levade took out her tarot deck, and they bent their heads once again over the table as they whispered, staring at the cards.

After she'd finished the reading, Levade made a rapid motion with her hands as if dusting them off in the air. Casey reached into her pocket, I assumed to pay Levade, but it appeared she handed her something instead, something small. I couldn't tell what it was, but I hoped it wasn't some personal girl-crush gift. Casey left hurriedly, and a tiny part of me was glad Levade hadn't turned her hand over and touched her palm, as she had mine.

Sass was waiting for me when I got home. He smacked up against me, and it felt good to have someone who was truly glad to see me and wanted to sleep with me, even if he was shedding.

CHAPTER FIFTEEN

The next evening, Judith the law professor stopped by the cabin to see if I'd be interested in a night-time swim, making good on her assertion that we needed more fun in our lives. She was wearing blue capri pants and a tight blue T-shirt and carrying what looked like scotch and water in a drink glass.

Apparently sensing my trepidation, she said, "I haven't taken a moonlight swim since I was a kid, but I know where all the sandbars and drop-offs are, so you'll be perfectly safe."

"I didn't bring a suit," I said.

"Even better! We'll skinny-dip. Haven't done that since my high school graduation." She slurred the word skinny, and that was enough to make me worry that she might try to swim drunk. For a split second I envisioned Marney staring out her cabin window at naked Judith lying on the shore, as I performed CPR on her, my butt-naked, skinny-dipping ass in the air. "Meet me down on our dock at midnight. Are you game?"

I snapped back to reality. "Sure." I was already deciding if a pair of shorts and a T-shirt would work as a makeshift swimsuit. I could always say I was cold.

❖

I locked the cabin, hid the key in the screen door, and walked down to the lake. Judith was in the water at the end of the dock paddling around when I arrived, which I thought was incredibly brave. What if I hadn't shown up and she dog-paddled to death? What if she bumped into bloated tourist bodies bobbing around in the dark? What if a sixty-five-pound muskie bit off her toes, mistaking them for minnows? Clearly, I wasn't the adventurous type, but I made up for it with a bizarre imagination.

"You're here!" she called out as I dumped my rubber flip-flops and started to wade into the water. "No, you don't! I'm out here buck naked, and I'm not swimming with a fully clothed person. Shrug the shorts."

I slung the towel over my shoulder toga style and slipped my shorts off behind the towel, then wrapped it around my waist and yanked my shirt off, tossing shirt and towel onto the beach only after I was sitting in the cold, shallow water. I had always been shy about my body, for no rational reason. Years without positive feedback, I thought. But I could give myself positive feedback.

"Are you afraid of leeches?" Judith laughed. "I wouldn't put my bare derriere on that clay in the dark."

"Ahhhh! I forgot." I dove out into deeper water to the harder sandy bottom and away from what kids used to call bloodsuckers. They were black or dark brown, and could be eight inches long and an inch wide, or they could be very tiny and hide in your bathing suit. Either way they "leeched" onto you like a suction cup. When pried off, they felt disgustingly gelatinous and left a small bruise where they'd attempted to suck blood. I was freaked by them as a child, and even more so as an adult.

I was no sooner out in the lake, flopping around naked, than a long, slender, black leech swam by. I shrieked and swam toward Judith, who caught me mid-stroke. "Well, I have worse news for you," she said, clutching my waist and holding me vertically in the water as we both dog-paddled. "You have one on your arm." I began thrashing around like a spastic chicken as Judith laughed. "Here, here. Settle down for a minute, and I'll pull it off." I closed my eyes and paddled, shivering in the cold water, as she plucked the leech off my arm and tossed it farther out into the lake.

"I've always loved Minnesota because there are no snakes, but I don't remember this many leeches when I used to swim here. I wish I'd brought an inner tube so I could get my legs out of the water."

"You're drawing them to you because you're afraid of them." She brushed against my chest and bent her knee, sliding it up between my legs, nesting it in my pubic hair and suspending me in the water. "You okay now?"

"I think my midnight swim is over."

"Too bad. I was kind of enjoying it. You have a very nice body," she said, like someone assessing a car. "Don't be so shy! Show it off."

"Thanks." I clambered onto the shore. As I was toweling off and yanking on my shorts, I caught a glimpse of a figure in white on the dock on the Point, facing our direction. My heart raced.

"I think I'll call it a night. Thanks for the leech rescue."

"I'll think of something more fun we can do. Take care."

I yanked on my T-shirt and flip-flops and covertly made my way through the woods to the Point, but the porch lights were out now, and I didn't see a sign of anyone.

Then I heard a scuffling sound inside and a male voice arguing with Levade. She opened the door and forcefully pushed the man out of her cabin. Small, tough, and bald as a pipe post, he tumbled down the front steps, and the dogs were on him in an instant, snarling and threatening to tear him apart, as he lay on the ground. He looked like the man with Frank on the island, the night I had dinner there with Levade.

"Don't ever rifle through my belongings again, Tony, and stay away from my cabin." She signaled the dogs to let him up.

Maybe there's a reason for Gus's trash talk in the tavern. Maybe Levade is somehow involved with everybody on the lake. I wanted to approach her and ask what was going on, but she'd already made me feel unwelcome, and this didn't seem like a moment that would change that. Besides, she seemed to be in control of her life, throwing a full-grown man out of her house.

I watched Tony get in his truck and drive off. Levade, the two dogs trailing her, went back inside, closed the door, and turned off the lights. Just the act of watching her leave made me sad. She's a complicated woman, I thought. There's just something about her—alone and so strong willed, fearless and outspoken, sexual and aloof, and I'm drawn to her and can't seem to help myself.

❖

As I started back through the woods, the wind picked up. I saw someone in the shadows on the path and stopped, my heart rate increasing. Frank appeared out of the dark, all in black with a hunting knife strapped to his belt. His mere presence completely terrified me.

"What are you doing out here this late at night?" he asked, obviously surprised to see me. I had a feeling his presence in the woods meant he was waiting for Tony. Otherwise his appearance was too coincidental, since he didn't live on the cove.

"Actually, what I'm doing is nobody's business," I said calmly.

"It is if you're sniffing around Levade's cabin." It was a different Frank. Not the man who gave expert tours, or the jovial fellow at the bear pits, but an angry man with an undercurrent of hatred, over what I had no idea. "What were you hoping to get there?" he asked, twitching and menacing, like he was working up to something he couldn't control. "Maybe this, huh?" He held my neck with his hand so he could kiss me. We were almost the same height, but he clearly outmuscled me.

"Get your hands off me!" I pulled back, and that response seemed to embolden him. I turned to run, and he grabbed my ankle, snagging me like a trip wire and forcing me to the ground, rolling me onto my back, and trying to rip my shorts off. My mind raced. *This is a man who's capable of wrestling a huge animal to its death.*

He held me by the throat with his left hand as he unzipped his pants with his right, pulled out his cock, and attempted to shove it into me. I screamed and fought back, scratching, clawing, and beating at his crotch, fighting with what little air I had left, as we tumbled across the forest floor.

My hand found a lake stone, and I grabbed it and hit him in the face. My voice was small and contorted as he choked off my air supply. "You rape me, and so help me God, I won't rest until I kill you."

He let up momentarily to check his facial wound. Realizing that I'd drawn blood, he laughed. Something about him found pleasure in pain, even his own pain, and he fought more viciously. The swirling wind blowing through the trees drowned out my cries for help, and for a moment I thought his raping me was the least of it. His rage might make him accidentally kill me.

Then a long, loud whoosh and the crack of wood, and pine needles descended like a blanket on us, followed by a massive tree limb crashing to the ground, hitting his shoulder. He sagged onto me, then rolled off to one side moaning, and I twisted and writhed and escaped. I didn't know if he got up off the ground and was following me, or if he'd come to his senses, but I ran like I'd never run before in my life and made it to the cabin. Shaking, I fumbled for the key and unlocked the door, then barricaded it and loaded the shotgun. I looked out the window at Marney's cabin, wondering if I should call her for help, but what could she do but wake Sam up, and what could Sam do but go ask Frank if he'd done what he would deny. *Besides if Frank breaks this door down, and I fire this gun, everyone will show up. No calls necessary.*

I slept with my shotgun loaded and beside my bed, thinking this is what women have been doing for centuries with men— running from them, hiding themselves and their children, and when all else failed, shooting them. But why was this happening to me now?

I've gone from being a woman who was verbally attacked by my ex-husband to being physically attacked by someone else's. The difference, I thought, is this time I'm forced to fight back.

CHAPTER SIXTEEN

I didn't sleep well until the sun began to rise. So the knock on the door startled me, and I got up disoriented. I took the gun with me and found Levade standing there.

"Let me in," she demanded, and I held the door open. "Show me where you're hurt."

"I don't really know. I haven't looked."

Levade walked me back to the bedroom, lifted my nightshirt, and looked me over, gently touching me, examining the cuts on my arm, and gasping over the bruise on my neck where his hand had clutched my throat.

"It was Frank, wasn't it?" Her voice was cold, and I nodded. Then I noticed I'd gotten blood on the sheets, and I asked her to give me a minute to clean up. I dashed into the bathroom and showered, and when I stepped out, she took the towel from me and gently patted places on my body that were scraped. Her touch was sensual, and if there had been no Frank, how wonderful this might have ended, with us in bed together, watching the lake, holding one another, and making love. But today I was too hurt, and she was upset and angry.

"How did you know he attacked me?"

"I didn't sleep. I had a bad feeling. Then this morning, I saw your face…you appeared to me, and I knew."

"I'm going into town to report him, as soon as I get dressed," I said, sticking with practicalities and avoiding the topic of how I "appeared" to her.

"You need to go back to New York. Nothing good will happen if you stay here."

"No. I'm not running away from someone like Frank."

"He will try to kill you, Taylor. I know this."

"I know all about Frank. He killed his wife over her lover. Well, he's not going to kill me. I promise you that."

My back, hips, and neck were sore, and just the act of pulling on my jeans, a shirt, and some tennis shoes was painful. I ran a brush through my hair, forgetting any makeup.

"I have to go."

"I'm going with you." She followed me to the car. "Give me your keys. I'll drive."

"I'm okay."

"Keys." She held out her hand, and I forked them over.

"You're demanding," I said lightly. "Living alone, you've learned to take care of yourself. Maybe you should let someone else take care of you on occasion. Just a suggestion."

She didn't reply.

It registered that it felt wonderful being in the car with her. Natural, in fact. Like I was home. *And what the hell does that mean? I'm a long way from home.*

The sheriff's office was also the police station, and as far as I could tell, it was also the jail and the courthouse, the latter two not in use that anyone could remember, unless it was to let a drunk sober up.

Judd and Robby Pierson were the volunteer-police department Sam had referenced. Judd was in his early-forties and dangerous looking, with facial scars and a strange grimace that never left. It would be hard to tell, if you didn't already know, which side of the law he was on, and in fact, I wasn't sure. He sat rocked back in Sam's chair with his feet up, pretending to be in charge.

Robby, his scraggly-haired brother, wore khaki pants and a khaki shirt, probably because it looked like a fake police-officer's uniform. He was all duck-strut and partridge chest, and he leaned up against the battered filing cabinet, posing as if he'd been voted Officer January in next year's police calendar.

As we entered, Levade whispered, "They're Frank's hunting and fishing buddies."

Judd spoke first. "What can we do for you two ladies?"

"Frank Tinnerson attacked me last night out by the lake. He tried to rape me."

Robby snorted and yanked on his pants, hoisting them higher, as if to say "old wild-man Frank" was always stirring up trouble.

"Did you get raped?" Judd asked.

"I fought him off," I said.

"So you're here to report a not-raped? Kinda like a boyfriend fight?"

"I'm here to report an attack, an attempted rape—"

"I don't know what riled him up," Robby said, "but I suspect you taught him his lesson, judging by the scratches on your arm there."

It dawned on me that, unfortunately, these two dumbasses could probably get a job on many a small-town police force, if they ever chose to leave here and stop being cops-for-free.

"She wants to file charges, Robby," Levade said.

"Any witnesses?" Robby asked, and I shook my head no. "Well, then, for all we know, you coulda done it to her, Levade."

"You are a dumb-fuck, Robby Pierson!" I'd never heard Levade resort to the kind of language I used regularly.

"Now, Levade, you of all people know Frank is the Teflon man, huh. Don'tcha? And this thing she's accusing Frank of is kind of like what that Blah-Blah Ford gal accused that fella of...you know, nearly raping her but didn't hit the target. Nobody seen it happen, so he got to be on the Supreme Court. That bein' the case, I don't think anybody would believe you, Levade, or you," Judd paused as if the word was hard to utter, "ma'am."

I asked for the forms to fill out that would allow me to file an official complaint. Robby hunted through the nearly empty file cabinet, obviously looking for something he knew didn't exist, and finally said, "All out of those forms. But I got a piece of paper here in the desk you can write on, and put it all down. And a pencil." He shoved the pencil toward me.

"You know, Robby, if Frank Tinnerson attacked your mom, or your sister, or a woman you loved, I would hope you would want it investigated," I said, trying to reason with the unreasonable.

Robby snorted. "Kind of an honor. Frank only likes the pretty ones."

"You can keep the paper and shove this pencil up your ass," I said calmly.

"One day Frank will be held accountable, as will you," Levade said.

"Now don't go threatening," Judd warned her.

"You gonna put the witchy-witchy on him, voodoo lady?" Robby giggled.

"Don't speak to her like that, ever, do you hear me?" I said evenly.

"Whoa, you two datin'...or somethin'?" Robby whistled.

Levade headed right for him, grabbed a hunk of his hair, and whipped his head to one side as if he were an out-of-control horse, and he yelped like he'd been stepped on. Judd jumped up to come to his rescue, and I grabbed Levade and pulled her away, just as Sam walked in the front door. The two men adopted a respectful tone.

"Morning, Sheriff." Judd stood tall. "These two ladies want to make a report about an attack last night by Frank Tinnerson." Then Judd excused them both, and they left the office to go do more of nothing, I assumed.

Levade was fuming. "He tried to rape her, Sam."

Sam shook his head as if this "Frank problem" was never ending. "You want me to go have a talk with him, tell him charges are being brought?"

She looked at me for answers. "You know him better than I do," I said.

"I do, and I know that he'll be on the loose while we try to prove he attacked you, and during that time he'll be even more dangerous," she said.

"She's right about that," Sam interjected.

"So he just gets away again?" I asked.

Sam let all the air out of his body as he contemplated his next move. "I'll go talk to him to let him know what we suspect, and I'll try not to get him too upset. He's not right, you know. The man's not right in the head."

Levade was angry. "He already knows we know what he did, because those two little weasel-helpers of yours are his fishing buddies, and right now they're off telling Frank that we came in here to file a report. And nothing will happen, because nothing in this town ever happens to protect women!" Levade grabbed me by the arm and pulled me outside to the car.

"You have to go back to New York."

"Well, I'm not going. And don't try to fight my battles for me. Let me handle this."

"You don't even know what you're fighting," she said quietly, and stared out the car window. What was going on in her beautiful head, and what would it take to get her to share it with me?

We drove in silence to the cabin and parked under the pines.

"What was so important that you agreed to meet with Frank in Pine City?" I was determined to get an answer.

"To warn him to stay away, for all the good that did."

"You were gone for days. You could have accomplished that in four hours."

Levade walked to the cabin with me. "I thought you and I needed a break."

"Why?"

"Because what's happening between us, Taylor, has to be serious enough to warrant the danger it puts us in, and I'm not sure you're that serious."

I opened the door, and we entered the kitchen. She looked into my eyes and said, "I am so sorry he attacked you." And she kissed me—a long, tender, sensual kiss that made me moan and buckled my knees.

"I feel I have to go on record that when you kiss me like that, I want to make love with you. But I've had a long talk with myself, and I don't want to make love to someone who wants me one minute and then is indifferent to me the next." That was what I needed to say, but then I quickly tried to lighten up. "Plus, you're younger and in better shape than I am, and further, you may be a little bit crazy or involved with people who are."

"So you're waiting for someone older, in poor physical condition, and boring? Is that the only thing keeping us apart?" Levade kissed me again. "We will be amazing together," she promised, and I nearly swooned at the thought of making love to her.

But the voice in my head would not be silent, and taking a deep breath, I summoned the courage to push her gently away. "Levade, you're involved in some way with Frank, and you won't tell me what's going on, despite the fact that he nearly raped me. I want romance with you, but without the drama. And for whatever reason, right now, you are nothing but drama. And you won't let me in so I can help you. I feel like we're both in a movie, but I'm not allowed to see the script."

"Drama can be temporary, but commitment is forever. I want your love forever, Taylor, in good times or bad. I want your love in addition to fabulous sex, not just sex. I'm not going to have another 'bridge love affair' to get me from here to the next relationship. The next time will be forever." She stared deep into my eyes. "For me, you're all or nothing." She paused and apparently read my mind, because she added, "And it feels like you might be nothing."

The final remark was cutting, and I started to hurl words back at her, but I refrained. Part of what she'd said was true. I wasn't committing to anyone and never had. And so I let Levade, the most amazing person I'd ever known, walk out of the cabin and out of my life, disappearing into the damp woods.

"She must be totally fucking crazy," I said to no one. "I haven't even had sex with the woman, and she wants a commitment forever. She wants to be lovers forever, soul mates. We hardly know each other!"

Sass slammed up against my leg and sauntered off to take a nap, obviously agreeing that one of us was crazy.

CHAPTER SEVENTEEN

Judith stopped by to invite me over for dinner that evening, having heard about the near-rape from Marney, who'd heard about it from someone in town who knew Judd and Robby. Everyone was undoubtedly eager for details, which I thought might have prompted Judith's spontaneous dinner invitation. Or maybe I was paranoid. Invitations did come late on the lake, and if you were already preparing dinner, then you put it in the fridge, and if you had company, then you brought them along. An opportunity for human contact was not to be passed up in a town with a tiny population.

I put on a pressed pair of designer jeans, a long-sleeved polo shirt tucked in at the waist, and tennis shoes. I looked trim and tidy and cabiny, but I felt oddly underdressed when Judith opened the door to greet me. Her hair was marcelled in rows of plastered black curls that rose and fell in tight waves against her head like a 1920s starlet. She wore an A-line skirt that hadn't been popular for decades, and a shirt with the sleeves rolled up to just below her elbow. Regardless, she was a law professor, so I was here for an evening of smart conversation, not a fashion show.

Dinner was meatloaf and mashed potatoes and a vegetable medley, which was a term used when there's not enough of one vegetable to warrant having its own name, so people start throwing in vegetable pieces and calling the thing a medley, as if it's so damned tasty it might burst into song. I'd never had a delicious vegetable medley, and tonight was no exception.

It quickly became apparent that Judith was looking for lust on the lake. She gave off the vibe of a woman on the hunt—eyes lingering longer than necessary, as if she was thinking something she wasn't saying, glances in my direction as if she was sharing some joke that hadn't yet been told. She found excuses to touch me and made it look coincidental to whatever she was doing, and she laughed at everything I said, regardless of whether it was funny or not.

After dinner, she told her mother about the attack I'd endured, and soon they were debating the political state of women, rape laws in various states, and Supreme Court decisions, as my head swung back and forth like the court judge at Wimbledon.

"If Georgia, Alabama, and the rest of the mouth-of-the-South legislators make abortion a crime, and women go to prison for ninety-nine years for ending a pregnancy, then Roe v. Wade is dead, and we're back to coat-hanger abortions. And that doesn't even address what happened to Taylor." She glanced away from her mother to quiz me. "He didn't penetrate you, did he?"

I was surprised by such a personal question and the look she gave me when she asked it. The possibility seemed to excite her, but maybe it was just the debate.

Judge Robertson said, "Attempted penetration is intent to rape. The fact that he failed in his attempt makes it no less a rape crime."

"Assault would be the charge," Judith insisted, and the two of them bantered as if I weren't there, perhaps energized by having an audience. I was bored and began looking out the window toward the Point when I thought they wouldn't notice, but I saw no light.

Finally Judith said she could tell they'd worn me out and insisted on walking me to my cabin in light of my recent attack. I told Judge Robertson what a lovely evening it was, even though it wasn't, and Judith and I crossed the cabin lawns to my place.

I could have sworn I saw Marney peeking out of her window as we strolled past. With her cabin situated between Judith's and mine, she had the perfect view and could hide and watch our travels back and forth, as we became her human version of a deer crossing.

"Sorry for cutting the evening short, but Mother leaves tomorrow morning. My brother is picking her up, and she'll be gone for a week, so she needs her rest. I'll have the cabin all to myself."

She stopped as we reached the birch trees, slid her arm around my waist, and suddenly pulled me in to her and kissed me. I was caught off guard, to say the least. The kiss wasn't precipitated by some signal on my part that I was interested in her, but more on logistics—her soon-to-be empty cabin and my availability. I didn't give Judith any sexual energy during our brief encounter, but she didn't seem to need it. She was overheated and behaving as if our chemistry were amazing.

"Tomorrow," Judith said in a guttural tone and ran her hand between my legs, then turned and left. Judith apparently did have a life beyond the buffet line, and I could end up being dessert.

Is every woman on the lake a lesbian? The water must have something in it besides leeches.

❖

Despite Judith's moonlight madness, all I could think about was Levade, standing in the kitchen, kissing me senseless, and telling me she wanted me forever and wanted me to want that too. It was still early in the evening. Maybe, if I went to her cabin, we could sit down, unemotionally, like two adults and just talk about what forever entails. Afterall, forever is a long word. Perhaps if I could have more time with her, ease into whatever she envisioned. *Maybe she knows things about our future together that I don't, and I'm just trying to catch up.* I decided to go see her and attempt to renew our relationship. At the very least, I'd like to rewind to that amazing kissing session on her couch.

I literally jogged over to the Point, taking the road behind the cabins to avoid Judith seeing me headed along the lakefront in that direction. Besides, after what had happened with Frank on the wooded trail, I was wary about taking that route in the dark.

Am I actually involved with two lesbians in one night? The lake water must alter your hormones.

In minutes I was on the north side of Levade's property, standing in her driveway. A car was parked there alongside her Jeep. Maybe someone getting a reading from her. I walked up the drive and whispered, "Hey, guys" to Charlie and Duke, who gave me a quick dog-sniff appraisal and then flopped back down on the lawn.

Across the screened porch, the living room was lit up and a small table set, and Levade and the woman from the horse show were having dinner. Levade seemed relaxed and was laughing, and she looked beautiful. The other woman appeared sophisticated and confident. Who is that woman? What is she doing here? If she's from Duluth, she had to drive hours to get to the Point, which means she's planning on spending the night. Well, obviously! The woman reached across the table and put her hand on Levade's arm and kept it there as she said something. Levade ducked her head, appearing shy but happy.

I felt like sagging to the ground and whimpering. I was jealous, no question about it. One minute Levade was stalking off because I wouldn't commit to her, and the next she was romancing some horsewoman. It's good you saw this, my inner voice told me. You were getting in too deep, and this is your wakeup call.

I patted Charlie and Duke good-bye and walked slowly back to my cabin, surprised that tears were running down my cheeks. *What the hell's that all about? If Levade is happy, then I should be happy. At least she's not alone. But now I'm alone, and I've never felt alone in my life.*

❖

At dawn, I heard a man's voice shouting from the van to the red cabin, asking for items that Judge Robertson had forgotten. "She needs her sleeping pills," the man yelled, and there was a pause as, presumably, Judith ran back for them. "Get a couple of baggies out of the kitchen, will you? And the brown sandals!" This went on for a while, and I got the giggles over how public it was and how strange the requests. "Animal Crackers on the counter!" That was the last thing I heard, proving she might be a judge, but she was also just an older lady who liked her cookies. The engine revved, and Judge Robertson shouted she'd be back in a week.

Literally half an hour later, I heard a knock at the back door, and Judith stood there in sweatpants holding a small thermos of coffee and two croissants. We drank and ate as I walked her around the cabin and answered questions about who'd owned it. Judith took big strides and waved her arms broadly, owning all the space around her. In fact, her mere presence seemed to shrink the cabin.

"My aunt Alice Armand and her husband Jake built it. Late in life, she sold it to her dear friend, who is also my publicist."

"Why did she sell it?" Judith set her coffee down on the window ledge, making herself at home.

"She said it made her sad and lonely." That memory popped out of my mouth, surprising me.

"We can't have this beautiful place remembered as sad and lonely!" She pulled me in to her again and gave me a long, hard French kiss that would have decked a Frenchman. Then she shoved her hand down my pants and grabbed all my anatomy in her large hand, squeezed it, and said, "Dinner tonight. I can't wait."

I jumped back as if I'd just discovered a snake in my pants. "I don't think I can come tonight, Judith."

Judith gave me a wicked grin. "I'll bet you can. And I have a surprise package for you. See you at six." Then she kissed me again, winked, and walked out the door.

Damn, I'm not attracted to this woman. But it's "a thing," kind of like bear-baiting, a once-in-a-lifetime opportunity that I've occasionally thought I wanted to experience. I'd had very lovely women in New York proposition me, but sitting across a table from them, both of us fully clothed, I just couldn't imagine it being any better than, well, Ben.

Regardless of the quality, sex with Judith might mean I could "try out lesbians" and not have to worry about emotional entanglements. For Levade's part, she'd made it clear she wasn't interested in a sexual relationship without my swearing allegiance to her for all eternity, and frankly that hadn't worked out so well for me. Ben came to mind.

And now Levade clearly has someone else, and probably always has had someone else. That romantic dinner didn't just happen spontaneously. This has been going on for a while, by the looks of it! So time for me to move on...I'm good at moving on... learning not to want what I can't have. So, I'm free to see whoever I choose, without any guilt over Levade, and Judith seems...well, logical. Then I thought about what I'd just thought, and I felt bad. Has it come to this, a "logical" romp in the hay?

It's the woods, I thought, blaming my outrageous behavior on a bunch of pine trees. *I'm with people I'll never see again, in the fucking forest, and presto, I'm into sexual experimentation, at forty-seven. That may be the unseemly part.*

The phone rang, and it was Ramona. She was correct. I was breathing a bit heavily, arguably because Judith had just taken an unexpected swan dive into my pants.

"What are you doing? Who are you doing? That woman, Levade?"

"Judith was here. The law professor from Minneapolis."

"Another woman? Are you seeing another woman?" When I giggled, she said, "You're a slut!"

"Ramona, do you think there's a chance I'm gay?"

"As opposed to confused or fucked up?"

"I'm being serious."

"I suppose it's always a possibility."

"Did you know that some studies say that women in their late forties have fluid sexuality and often find themselves transitioning out of heterosexual marriages and into same-sex relationships late in life?"

"You're spending an inordinate amount of time researching this topic."

"Let's see," I said, only slightly tongue in cheek. "I could enjoy being belittled, picking up his underwear off the floor, pretending I had an orgasm when it was more like genital rug burn, and cooking ten thousand dinners, or I could have a soft, sensual woman make love to me. Which would you choose?"

"Honey, I'm hard-core penis. All they have to do is open the door for me, protect me from snakes, and not fart in bed."

"Why didn't you tell me I could be gay?"

"There's a lot of things I haven't told you." And she didn't laugh.

CHAPTER EIGHTEEN

Judith's cabin was the most poorly decorated of the ones Marney rented out. The walls were pine boards painted cabin-red, and here and there anachronistic, dime-store art hung at cockeyed angles throughout the living room—the ruins of Pompei on a thin canvas, a faded chuckwagon scene from the 1800s captive in a plastic frame, and a football-shaped plaque that said, GO BADGERS! It was a cabin, appropriately enough, having an identity crisis. *This place is so boring it could actually benefit from a coat of white paint and a salt-and-pepper shaker of two copulating coyotes.*

On the tiny patio, overlooking the lake, Judith was grilling burgers and making pleasant conversation about her home in Minneapolis and her dog, Wolfgang, whom she missed but couldn't bring to the cabin, because he got distracted and chased squirrels. Me too, I thought.

I had barely finished eating when she began doubling up on the wine. Foreplay wasn't exactly her strong suit. She tried holding my hand under the table during dinner, ruffling my hair as she cleared dishes, and then plopping down beside me on the couch, her arm draped over my shoulder, so she could rub my breast, all while asking me if I liked living in New York.

It seemed awkward, and I was clearly no help, because I was still trying to decide why I was even contemplating sex with

Judith. *Is it to get back at Levade? That would be infantile. Is it to get over Levade?* I paused on that one, having to admit that losing Levade to the equestrian-creature was painful, because I felt emotionally attached to her, more emotionally attached than I'd ever allowed myself to be toward anyone. And that in itself is ridiculous, I thought.

I had to get Levade out of my head because Judith was right there in front of me, and it was obvious she wanted to race through the niceties as quickly as possible and rush to the bedroom. Within minutes, she was towing me in that direction. The small bedroom was cabinesque, with narrow pine-slat walls, a small bed covered in a well-worn quilt, and a rustic dresser with a bear-lamp on it. She kissed me several times and then suggested I get comfortable, and she'd be right back.

While taking off my clothes, I mused that this must be lesbian sex at forty-seven—no intrigue, no foreplay, just prepare to be fucked. I was sorry I'd gotten myself into this situation, and, frankly, I wished I could just call the whole thing off. *This is truly an ill-conceived experiment and beneath me.* I even contemplated doing my retching trick that had worked on Frank, but before I could launch into a pretend-puke performance, I heard her leave the bathroom, and seconds later, she appeared in the bedroom doorway naked.

I hadn't really seen her body during the infamous midnight swim, but now I had the full view and thought she looked better naked, without the 1940s clothes. A pretty face, small firm breasts, a narrow waist, and then my eyes traveled south. She was wearing a velvet harness around her waist with straps extending down and around each leg. On closer examination, at crotch level, I realized part of the apparatus held a strap-on dildo that seemed partially erect. The harness appeared custom fitted to carry two additional smaller dildos that were thankfully "at rest," kind of like Snap-on tools, in case size was a problem. She braced herself in the doorway with arms outstretched, head cocked, and pelvis jutting forward.

"Surprise package! Can you handle this, baby?"

"Oh, my God!" I don't know what came over me, but I burst out laughing, and the more offended she became, the more I laughed.

"I find this an odd and somewhat insulting reaction," she said, slouching a bit in her full-regalia genitalia.

"I'm so sorry, Judith. It's just that I've been with men all my life, so I've seen all manner of penises. Never three on the same person, I grant you, but for whatever reason, none of them excited me. Nonetheless, they were all the real deal. So I decide to take a foray into lesbian sex and meet a woman, a very nice and lovely woman, wearing an entire set of rubber penises." I began laughing again. "Life is so ironic."

She took a step forward and then launched herself into the air, landing on me and flattening me like a WWF wrestler, then quickly covered my mouth with hers, probably to shut me up. I pushed her away so I could breathe, and she tried to penetrate me with her dildo. It was rough sex with strange toys. "Judith, hold it. Stop it! Let me up."

When she realized I was serious about leaving, she made a last-ditch effort to save the evening, grabbed the harness, ripped it off her body, and flung it across the room. The larger rubber penis bounced off the wall and landed on the bear-lamp, sticking out of the top like a foreskin finial.

"I get it," she said, still trying to have sex with me. "I know a local guy, good-looking and clean, and he loves threesomes."

"Not my thing." I pushed her off me again. "This doesn't work for me. Not your fault," I said, in the way I said it to men, when in effect it was their fault. "It's just too complicated."

I grabbed my clothes as she kissed my back and tried to convince me to stay, but I was out the door and across the lawn in an Olympic sprint. Sass scattered as I blew through the door. "Pussy!" I panted to the terrified feline. "Stay away from it!"

❖

The next day the older boy I'd seen playing pool at Jensen's passed me on the sidewalk, as I was getting out of my car in front of the hardware store, and he gave me a wink and a low wolf whistle. Was this kid the one Judith was calling for the threesome? I was paranoid and remorseful. *This is what happens when you have no relationship for four years—well, virtually no relationship.*

I was so depressed that I did what all good women do in a stressful situation. I stopped at the drugstore soda fountain and ordered a chocolate sundae. Casey, the freckled teenage version of Emma Stone, served it up.

"That bad?" she asked slyly.

"Looking for love in all the wrong places."

"This whole town would be the wrong place, so I hope it's not here." She pushed strands of her strawberry-blond hair back behind her ear.

"You're pretty savvy. Aren't you just out of high school?"

"Yeah, but it's a small town. You see it all because you know everybody."

"You have a boyfriend?"

"Used to."

"Mind if I ask what happened?"

"He was into summer threesomes with some woman who was renting Jensen's cabin every year. He thought it was all fine because it paid well. He's a jerk."

I blushed, thinking about who that woman might be. "I saw you going to the Point for a reading," I said, happy to change the subject.

The fact that I knew she'd been there seemed to upset her. "That wasn't me. You must have seen someone else."

"Could be." I thanked her for the ice cream and left. Why would she lie about visiting Levade?

I crossed the street to the hardware store and noticed, through the glass storefront, that Gladys, the owner, was behind the counter talking to Little Man, showing him some knives from the case. I was surprised that a Native American with access to an entire tribe of artisans wouldn't just have the tribe make him a knife, which made me think that Nordic craftsmanship must be revered in this part of the country. I got in my car, making a mental note to go back to the hardware store and have a look at the artisanry when I had more time.

I turned on the radio, and the announcer, in a thick Norwegian accent, was welcoming listeners to the twenty-four-hour polka station, as he cued up the "Beer Barrel Polka." What kind of loon listens all day to polka music? I thought, tapping my hand on the steering wheel and bobbing my head in time to oom-pa-pa and tra-la-la and somebody rolling out a barrel, surprised that, before I knew it, I'd polka-ed my way back to the cabin.

CHAPTER NINETEEN

I dumped my dirty clothes into the ancient washing machine while I spent time working on the book. The female lover was completely captivated by the ex-wife, whom she realized she could never have. Their worlds were too far apart, their experiences too diverse, their relationship too painful. But if she couldn't have her, she was committed to protecting her from the man she'd once loved, who was determined to kill her.

I heard the old washing machine make a whop-whop-whop sound and then flop to a stop. I jumped up and piled the wet clothes into a wicker basket containing clothespins and headed out to the clothesline, where I pinned jeans, T-shirts, and underwear up on the line, watching them flap in the wind. I smiled at the thought that a place still existed where you had to wash clothes on a day when the breeze was strong and there was no rain, pin them up, and then remember to go get them before tree sap and bugs adhered to them or rain set in.

When I rounded the corner with my empty clothes basket, Judith was sitting on the back steps.

"What are you doing here?" I asked.

"Waiting for you. I want to start over."

I felt bad for her. However she chose to have sex was fine. We just weren't a match. "We can be friends, Judith, but I'm not up for anything else."

"Of course we can be friends. We *are* friends." She jumped up and wrapped her arms around me. I pushed her away decisively, but she wasn't giving up that easily. "I read you wrong. I thought you wanted a little fun in the sun, sport sex, and see what develops."

She was right about the signals I was sending out by going to her cabin for burgers, knowing full well I was bringing the buns. I was just "trying out lesbian sex," which wasn't fair, and frankly, I would criticize that behavior if anyone else did it.

"I'm sorry," I said, but that didn't change the fact that I'd already experienced it and didn't want to experience any more.

"You can't reject me over one rocky evening."

As she tried to convince me to let her inside the cabin, a car pulled into the drive, one I didn't recognize. The door opened and my jaw dropped.

"Ramona!" I shouted, as if she'd just found me at the bottom of a well after a week missing. She waved wildly, seeming to assess my dilemma, and made a beeline toward me.

"Darling, it's so good to see you." And she kissed me, dropping her big Louis Vuitton bag on the porch, signaling ownership of the territory and her intent to stay a while, and she looked fabulous in black. "I've missed you!"

"What are you doing here?" I asked.

"I had business in Chicago and thought how could I not come see you." Her tone was just a tiny bit provocative, and I realized she was loving my dilemma.

"Ramona, this is Judith. Judith, my dearest friend and publicist, Ramona Ryder." Judith shook hands but was already backing away, clearly trying to determine the relationship Ramona represented.

"Nice to meet you." She broke eye contact with Ramona to give me a look. "I hope we'll see more of each other, Taylor." And she was gone across the lawn.

"How much of you has she seen so far?" Ramona quipped.

"You saved me. Come in. I'm so glad you're here."

"You look fetching with your little clothes basket under your arm. I expected you to break into four bars of "Oklahoma."

"If you'd break down and buy a dryer, I could be less 'fetching.'" I shot her a look.

"No dryer is part of the charm."

Ramona slung off her jacket on entering and eyed the place with a quick swish-pan of her head. "I'm staying one fucking night in these woods to get you out of trouble." She plopped down in the rocker and produced a small, silver flask of whiskey. "What an abysmal flight and drive. No wonder people never leave here. It's just too taxing."

"Who said I was in trouble?" I backtracked.

"Marney, who met me in town for coffee this afternoon before I drove out. She was a veritable font of information. She has guilt over introducing you to Judith. She didn't know Judith was gay, and she doesn't want to be responsible for 'turning you into gay,' as she put it. She also snooped in the red cabin while they were doing the housekeeping and found a rubber dick stuck in the lamp." She waited for a response and, when she didn't get one, kicked off her heels. "I don't need one of my authors generating bad press with lesbians and other people's husbands."

"What other people's husbands?"

"Ralph got caught in his drowning-boy-rescue story, so he threw you under the bus. Said he was trying to get away from you."

"Oh, my God. Marney must hate me!"

"Marney's got Ralph's number. The lying little lard bucket can barely swim, so he couldn't rescue a drowning teenager in a wading pool, much less the lake." She glanced over at Sass's litter box. "Is that a wading pool?"

"Kind of. Yes."

She got up to retrieve a glass and some ice. "You're thin and tan. You look great. No wonder that Judith-woman is chasing you.

Don't let me forget that I've got a contract from your publisher out in the car, for the book you're writing." She arched an eyebrow, letting me know she'd told my publisher I was writing, and therefore I'd better be writing. "She also asked me to get a picture of you so she can be reminded of what you look like," she said slyly.

Someone knocked on the door, and Ramona said, "Let me handle her." She walked to the door, and from across the room I could see Levade standing there, managing to look amazingly gorgeous at all hours of the day in her shorts and polo shirt.

"Well, hello!" Ramona said in an appreciative tone.

Levade took one look at Ramona and turned, saying over her shoulder, "I'm sorry this isn't a good time. I'll come back."

I bolted from my chair, pushed Ramona aside, and ran down the steps calling out to her, but she had already disappeared into the woods. I returned breathless and despondent.

"My God, you're like some horn-toad teenager. Was that Levade?"

I nodded.

"Well, you're right. She's gorgeous!" Ramona playfully sang the refrain to "Sister Golden Hair." "1975, America."

"Is that the last year you remember any music?"

"Maybe I should stick with real lesbians. They're not as snarky as straight women trying to make the transition."

Sasquatch had heard Levade's voice and bounded into the living room. Ramona yelped, jumped back into her chair, and tucked her feet up under her. "My GOD, that's a big cat!"

"And he sleeps on my head," I said.

"Are you sure he's not a lynx or something?" she asked, keeping her eyes on him.

"He's a cat."

"I had no idea they made them that large."

I tried to get Ramona to let me cook something or make her a sandwich. She said she'd eaten and just sipped her whiskey.

"So in addition to saving your ass, I really came up here to share some things with you that I thought would be more interesting in person."

"Are you okay? Is your health okay?"

"I am in magnificent health," she said. "You brought up Maynard, and how he went on about your Uncle Jake seeing his wife."

"Aunt Alice must have been so embarrassed."

"No. She was so relieved because your aunt Alice was having a love affair with Angelique Bisset, the equestrian woman on the Point."

"Nooo!"

"They met in their late forties and for thirty years spent every summer together here, meeting clandestinely. I was Alice's dear friend and their 'beard,' passing messages and going out with them sometimes, so people would think we were just girls looking for men, when in fact only one of us was. I've never seen two people more in love." She paused to take a sip from her chic little flask. "They were just happy to be together. They needed no one else. Here." She reached into her bag and pulled out a yellowed envelope.

Inside were three pictures—one with Angelique standing next to Alice with her arm around her, Angelique significantly taller. The second photo showed the two of them bareback on a white horse—Alice, in a white linen dress, her arms wrapped around Angelique's waist and her face pressed against her back as if they were riding off into the sunset, leaving every care behind them. And the third was of Angelique reclining on the porch swing out on the Point, Alice leaning back in her arms, both looking very much in love. "I took these, of course," Ramona said softly.

"Oh, they're so beautiful together. It makes me sad that they lived apart. Why didn't Aunt Alice just leave Jake?"

"In a way he was great cover, and in those days, women needed cover." She held up the third photo of the two of them in the swing so I could see it again. "This is what love looks like, darling. And great sex. They were in bed constantly!" She laughed a raucous laugh.

I grabbed the postcard off the desk. "I found this in the desk drawer."

"That's Alice's handwriting. She said the flourish on the *L* was her secret code for 'I love you.'"

My heart stopped. The note on the screen door at Levade's cabin saying she had to leave and hoped I was inspired had that same *L* on it. I must have been floating out in the stratosphere contemplating the joy of that secret message, when Ramona snapped her fingers and brought me back to the present.

"I haven't been here long enough to cause you to leave your body."

"Sorry. It's the *L* for 'I love you,'" I said dreamily, thinking of Levade, but Ramona thought I was talking about Aunt Alice.

"I know. Isn't that sweet? She obviously meant this postcard for Angelique but didn't get to send it. When Angelique died, Alice said it was too painful to come back here, but she didn't want the cabin to go to a stranger, so I bought it."

I let this news rumble around in my head. From a child's perspective, she was my loving old aunt who cared for kids, and cooked, and laughed, but behind all that she was so much more she couldn't share. "Aunt Alice had a lesbian lover who was the woman on the Point who is now the ghost."

"I don't know about the ghost part, but yes. I brought a letter I found in Angelique's things right after she died."

I took the letter out of her hand and read it out loud.

I have never wanted anything or anyone more than I want you. When I'm touching you, I am in heaven. When you're inside me, I am whole. When you are gone, I am desolate. Come back to me soon.

Loving you forever, Alice.

"Pretty hot, yes? Ramona grinned.

"Wow, Aunt Alice." I sighed.

As if giving me lessons, Ramona said, "And that's what love sounds like." She hoisted herself out of the chair. "Wait, there's more, but it might require food."

She headed for the bathroom, and I slung together a ham-and-cheese sandwich and some chips, taking it to her in the living room.

"I saw the quilt on your bed in there, the one with the horse squares. I remember when Alice made that, so she'd always sleep under something that reminded her of Angelique."

Loving her so much she wanted to sleep beneath the quilt that was a reminder of her, how lucky the two of them were to have found each other. I sighed.

Ramona was on to a different subject, talking as she chewed. "So you know that Levade is Angelique's niece?"

I nodded.

"Well, rumor has it that Levade had an affair with Frank Tinnerson's wife."

"Levade is the woman who had an affair with Frank's wife and got her murdered?" My heart nearly stopped. "Why would she do that? She must have known how crazy Frank is!"

"After what you've done, you can't hold that against her."

My mind was buzzing. "How long were they together? Why would she have an affair with his wife?"

"I've told you all I know, and I have a plane to catch tomorrow. Let me read the first chapter tonight…the first paragraph even."

"I've got nothing," I lied, preferring not to allow piecemeal readings of my work, and waved a blank sheet of paper in the air for emphasis, while still upset that Levade had had an affair—apparently an intense one, to risk Frank's discovering it.

Ramona admonished me. "You have to balance writing and fucking. Great fucking can make great writing. Too much fucking makes no writing, and you're fucked. I have a contract in the car, for God's sake!"

I put her to bed in the bedroom off the living room and then sat for hours, propped up on the pillows in my bed, staring out at the reflection of the moon on the lake and thinking about Levade having an affair with Frank's wife. I was agitated and angry.

Maybe if I could have her, make love to her, I could think again. *Although wanting her has put passion back in my soul and enabled me to write. Is that all she is to me—lust and a literary muse?* But in my heart, I knew it was much more. Secretly, I believed Levade had put the *L* on her note to say she loved me; and Angelique had put the *L* on the opposite side of the card to remind me of that fact, and to tell me not to give up. It might just be a story I was making up, but I held that story close to my heart.

❖

We were awakened early by a knock at the door. I ran to open it, hoping it was Levade, and was startled to see Frank there, draped over the porch rail, swaggering while slouching, if that were possible.

"Frank, you're not to come by any more, and if you continue to do it, I'll call the sheriff."

"Ohhh, the sheriff." He gave me a mock-terrified look. "Speaking of which, Sam stopped by and told me you'd showed up at his office to complain about me, and you were real upset about what happened the other night." Frank was clearly communicating that nothing happened in these woods that he didn't know about and control. "Anyway, I thought I'd better come by and offer an apology," he said, his tone derisive.

"Leave!"

"Just so you know, I like a woman who fights back. Truthfully, I don't know what came over me. Must be you smell so good, and you're so soft. I never met anyone as soft as you."

"Get the hell off this property. I have a gun and I will shoot you, Frank."

"Heard you got a gun. Guns are dangerous. My poor, loving wife could tell you that." He sauntered off. Ramona was behind me when I turned around.

"I don't know why he's focused on you, but you need to get the hell out of here."

All I could think of was Levade in bed with Frank's wife. "I think he needs to get the hell out of here," I said, surprised at the steel in my voice.

❖

Ramona was packed and finishing her coffee, and I hated to see her go. Obviously worried and sad at leaving me, she reached for levity. "The damned cat came to see me last night and slept on my head."

"I should have locked him in my room. Sorry."

"It was nice actually. I felt like a member of the Queen's Royal Guard with his long, furry paws hanging down around my neck like chin straps. We've become very close. Just don't let him claw the damned couch."

She hugged me good-bye, patted Sass, and was headed back to what she called "civilization."

"Why did you buy this cabin if the woods freak you out?" I asked.

"I'm more sentimental than you know. Besides, you can own something you're not, if it helps you give up something you are."

"Wow. Who knew you were that deep," I teased. "I don't even think I know what the hell that means."

"I love you too. Write something, will you?"

CHAPTER TWENTY

R amona had no sooner driven off than I put on my jeans and headed through the woods to the Point. I was hurt and mad and feeling like a whole lot was going on that put both Levade and me in danger, and I wanted answers.

I banged on the screen door, and Levade appeared in her nightshirt, which knocked the anger right out of me. She had obviously just gotten out of bed. This is how she looks when she first wakes up, I thought, wishing I could wake up beside her.

"Why didn't you come in?" I asked.

"You had company."

"Well, so did you. Who was the horsewoman you were dining with the other night? Why don't you just have the decency to tell me you're seeing someone?"

A smile played on Levade's lips. "That woman was here to ask me to head up the dressage chapter in our area."

"And she had to grasp your arm and spend the night in order to get that done?"

"I am not involved with her, Taylor. But, speaking of guests, who was the attractive older woman answering your cabin door yesterday?"

"That's my publicist from New York, and I'm staying in her cabin. She came all the way across the country to tell me things you might have shared with me and saved her the trip.

"Such as?"

I pushed the screen open and walked across the porch and into the house as if I owned the place. "Well, for starters, my aunt Alice and your aunt Angelique were lovers—"

"Soul mates," she said softly.

"For thirty years."

"Yes."

"And you had an affair with Frank's wife."

"No, I didn't. She came to me for readings and advice, because he beat her so badly on a couple of occasions. Ultimately the fact that she came to see me got her killed. He accused her of an affair with me, but that wasn't true."

I relaxed a little, feeling possessive of her and now able to release the picture of her in bed with another woman.

"Then who was Frank's wife seeing?"

"Dolores was seeing a woman at the tavern...Kay."

I stopped to contemplate that information. So Kay, the woman who bought me a glass of wine in this goldfish-bowl town, was making a living in a bar where the owner belittled women and where her lover, Dolores, was murdered by her husband, and the murderer was still walking around being a big-shot, sport-fishing celebrity.

"Is Kay afraid of him?"

"The last time I saw her, I got the sense that she was growing stronger. She just wants him to pay for what he did."

"So Frank won't allow you to have a relationship because he doesn't want you to have someone when he doesn't? Or is he just a crazy rapist, or a murderer, or what?"

"Frank is my stepbrother."

Goose bumps ran up my arms, and my jaw slackened.

Levade walked out on the porch and sat down at the table where she did her card readings, and I followed. To provide me with answers, she gravitated to the place where she got most of hers.

"When I was eight," she sighed, beginning slowly, "I told our parents he had molested me. His father, my stepfather, didn't believe me, and he and my mother fought over it often. Finally, she sent me to live with my aunt. That move changed my life, because one day Angelique let me ride her horse, which she never allowed anyone to do. It was in that moment that I felt stronger and more powerful than I ever had, like no one could hurt me. The horse gave me his power until I could find my own." She paused for a moment, and I started tearing up. "After I left home, my stepfather beat Frank, and then ultimately he divorced my mother. Frank has always tried to harm anyone or anything I love because of what happened. He blames me for breaking the family apart."

"And what did your mother say about what Frank did to you?"

"By the time I was old enough to know I wanted to have a conversation with her about it, she'd developed Alzheimer's, so most of the time she thought I was her nurse."

I took her hands in mine, clutching them as if I would never let her go, and the tears that had welled up in my eyes spilled over onto my cheeks. Having her stepbrother molest her, her family reject her, her parents blame her for their divorce, and her stepbrother still torture her, no wonder she kept to herself physically and emotionally. *And no wonder she wants someone who will be with her forever. She has no one.*

"I want to protect both you and Alizar from him," I said, and although I felt that pledge in my heart, I also felt a gentle breeze move across my right ear, as if Angelique was whispering to me, telling me what to say, and making me say it out loud. That sensation was both crazy and oddly comforting.

Levade stood up and began nervously pacing. "Frank will never let me alone. He said he moved here for the fishing and because Dolores was from here, but it was primarily to keep an eye on me. He made a name for himself. He's protected here. He's a champion fisherman, the man other men call Crazy Frank the Muskie Man, but they still want to live vicariously through him. He's the guy who outsmarts everyone and gets away with anything. And that's why he's so dangerous."

"A sick, cowardly killer—that's all I see when I think of him." I reached for her and pulled her close, but she stiffened.

"What were you doing with that woman in the red cabin?"

I was caught off guard and searched for a plausible explanation. "You didn't seem to want me. I needed to find out if anyone would."

Levade's cheeks reddened, and her eyes were wet and hot. "Don't ever lie to me, Taylor. I don't have to literally see things to know things."

That's a frightening thought! "I wanted to know what lesbian sex was like." There, I'd told her the truth.

She shoved me away from her. "What are you doing, TJ?" No one had called me by my nickname since I was a kid in Missouri. "You're treating the most intimate experience two human beings can have as if it's all about shoe size'"

"Give me a break. I've gone from being a hard-core heterosexual to being, well…involved with you. From being completely unemotional about sexual relationships to being pretty obsessed with you. So I think I just need a little training."

"I train horses, not idiots."

"I'm not an idiot. I don't let anyone call me that." My face was hot.

"You're right. You're not an idiot. You just behave like one."

"Angelique obviously doesn't think so, and she wants us to be together. I think she picked me out for you."

"I told you she and I have different taste in women."

"You haven't even tasted me to know that." I smiled at her, and this time she reddened and glanced away. "Look, I know you're freaked over Frank, and for good reason. We'll deal with it. I wish your aunt would just get rid of him." I was only half joking. "And while we're seeking otherworldly help, where's *my* aunt?"

Levade smiled. "Alice is with Angelique. They're here in the wind." I could feel the wind kicking up even through the screen, and its presence was sexually arousing.

I tried to get close to Levade again. "I'm here in the wind too."

Her voice sounded cold. "Then you might want to blow over to the red cabin, where someone gives a shit." She went back in the house and slammed the door. I backed off the porch and tumbled down the steps. *These damned cabin steps are deadly. She isn't even checking to see if I'm hurt. She's not someone to get involved with.*

"I twisted my ankle, and I don't need this shit!" I shouted. "And the cat is better off with me. A more stable environment!" As I got to my feet and limped back to the cabin, my ankle torqued and throbbing, I lectured myself. What in the hell have I gotten myself into? A teenage shouting match! It must be the lake causing it, like Maynard said. Warm sun, waves lapping up against you, pine trees whispering to you, and pretty soon…bang…you've turned into a fucking lesbian!

❖

Sasquatch must have had a bigger house with his former owner, or the run of a backyard, or more attention than I was giving him, because he was obviously getting cabin fever, picking up paws-full of peanuts right out of the bag and throwing them across the room, shredding the toilet-paper roll, racing around the house intentionally sliding into the furniture, toppling lamps, and sometimes just howling.

I swept the floor because he was throwing kitty litter out of his wading pool like he was planting corn. I cracked the back door to toss the debris out, and Sass blew through the tiny opening, moving so fast he was just a flash of fur headed for the woods. I flew after him on my weak ankle. *If he's eaten by a bear, I will sob, after which Levade will kill me. Or if Frank finds him, he will kill him and stuff him and use him as a doorstop.*

My shouting brought Marney and Judith out of their cabins, and they quickly joined in the hunt. Marney peeked around trees, baby-talking, "Here kitty-witty-Sassy-frassy!" Judith shouted, "Here, Sass. Come on, Sass!" And I screamed, "God damn it, Cat. Get your ass back here before you're shot and fucking stuffed!" Apparently, Judith's approach was the preferable one, because within a few minutes she rounded the corner, the large feline pressed to her chest, and she deposited him in the kitchen.

"Oh, my God, thank you!" I hugged her and thanked Marney, waving her off.

"Pussy delivery," Judith said, giving me the eye as she dusted the hair off her shirt and then immediately began pawing me, trying to pick up where we'd left off, saying she wanted a night together.

I don't know if it was anger over being rejected by Levade, or the pain in my twisted ankle, or the ridiculous circumstances of life, but I was not in the mood for Judith, while at the same time I was in her debt for the Sass-catch.

"Listen to me, Judith." I tried to be low-key and kind. "I just can't get interested in a dip with a rubber dick, regardless of who it's attached to. And although I'm sure your factory-installed equipment is lovely, I just want to stop having sex for sex's sake. It's not rewarding, and it makes me feel bad. Does that make sense?" I didn't give her time to answer. "I want to write and be left alone. You need to find a nice, normal woman to sleep with, and live with. You're smart and talented, and it's time to trade in the trapeze for a porch swing. I'm sorry if I offended you, or used you, or led you on, but I just need to break this off."

"Wow! You have issues. All this bullshit over sex toys? That's why straight women are such a pain in the ass. Of course I use sex toys! Because my bedroom is more fun than yours. You marry some guy, and whatever he's dangling is all you get. And now, thanks to your prude-tude, I have four days of an empty cabin. Had I known you were a walking basket case, I would have lined up someone else!" She stalked back across the lawn to her cabin as Marney watched through her window.

"Lined up?" I screamed so Judith could hear me. "What are you, a booking agent? You know who books sex? Pimps and hookers! Otherwise it's called dating! And you don't show up on a first date wearing a fucking tool kit!"

I could see the whites of Marney's eyes clear across the lawn.

❖

I tried to write, but my blood pressure was up, and my throbbing ankle needed attention, so I headed to Jensen's juke joint for whatever pain relief they had on hand. I was entering the front door just as Judith was walking out the back with a six-pack of beer. My God, this town is so small, you can't fart without someone opening a window.

I looked at the limited array of balms. *Ben Gay.* Done that, I thought.

A silver-haired woman in jeans and a biker vest, who sat at the bar, drunk out of her mind, spotted me and stage-whispered, "I knew your uncle real well. He and I used to get it on when your auntie wasn't around. Wilma Swensen." She extended her hand, causing her to lose her balance and nearly topple off the bar stool.

"So you're Wild-Wilma, who fucked Jake, Rake-of-the-Lake." I enjoyed giving her a double descriptor.

"Your aunt didn't know how to handle a man like Jake."

"My aunt didn't want to handle him because she was madly in love with someone else, and she was happy that Jake was stickin' his dick in a drunk lake chick! Let's drink to that!" I made an air-toast while Wilma apparently tried to decide if she was being insulted or celebrated.

"You tell 'em, Willie," one of the boys at the pool table shouted, goading her. Wilma was emboldened. "We got it on almost as good as you and that professor did. She was here a minute ago." That put a cork in my cleverness. *Were there cameras in the cabin, or did Judith tell the boys, or the whole damned place, what had happened?*

"Whatever she told you didn't happen," I said under my breath.

"Of course, honey. That's what we all say." She gave me a raspy barroom laugh as she patted me warmly on the arm.

I paid for Icy Hot and two reusable ice packs and walked out the back door and through the woods, rather than take the winding highway home. I heard male voices and a twig snap, then laughter and men stumbling through the woods.

"Hey, Taylor. Talk to us. Come on now." They laughed and shrieked and giggled like girls. They were having fun taunting a woman, but I was terrified and ran as if I were being chased by a pack of wolves that could encircle me and tear me apart. *Do I have to start taking my shotgun to Jensen's, for God's sake?*

By the time I got home, my ankle had turned a brighter purple, and I crawled into bed. Sasquatch had settled back into being a house cat after his run through the woods. He curled up next to me, and after a few minutes I picked him up and draped him over my head.

"Let's stick to our routine. I've had all the change I can take."

CHAPTER TWENTY-ONE

The first draft of the book was wrapping up. A twist in plot had finally allowed the wife to escape her stalking ex-husband and to realize love in the form of the woman she had only dreamed about. But would her lover feel the same, and would it last?

It was late in the afternoon when I put the manuscript to bed, and I decided to celebrate, taking a glass of wine down to the dock and dangling my feet, and my nearly healed ankle, in the clear, icy, lake water, staring at the most peaceful scene imaginable. Despite what was going on inside me, the lake was calm.

A few minutes later, I heard a screen door slam in the distance. Sounds carried like musical notes along the quiet lakeshore. Teens laughing, motors buzzing, doors slamming, they were all muted and distant, reminding you that people were around, but it would take them a while to reach you.

Soon, over my left shoulder, I spotted Judith headed my way, working her way down the hill. I casually took my feet out of the water and dried them off on a towel, preparing to leave, as she shouted, "Keep your pants on. I'm here for détente." She'd obviously been watching me, because she'd brought her own wineglass.

I put my feet back in the water as a gesture of peace. She walked the dock planks that bounced with her every step and plopped down next to me, putting her feet in the cold lake beside mine.

"We live too close to be aggrieved lovers," she said.

"We were never lovers." I smirked.

"And I'm completely over you." She punched me with her right shoulder, and we both laughed, since we knew she'd never had any real feelings for me in the first place.

"So Marney tells me you spend a lot of time down at the Point," she teased.

"Marney has turned us all into a soap opera for her viewing entertainment."

"Are you attracted to the woman who lives there?" she asked, feigning mild interest as she splashed her feet, making noise and spraying water. "Well, are you?" She intentionally splashed water up onto my shorts, and I shrieked.

"Why are you asking me that?" I laughed.

"I'm just here, therapist of the pines, and thought I'd offer a little friendly lesbian advice. That's all." She intentionally said nothing more.

"You're going to make me beg for this advice?"

"No. But if you don't, you won't get it." She paused and cut me a mischievous look. "And it's damned good advice, because I've been at this decades longer than you have. But then if you don't need it, I understand. We all have our own styles." She pulled her feet out of the water.

"Okay, spill it. Please."

"You're not forceful enough," she said flatly.

I burst out laughing. "Oh, forceful like you, Don Juan of the Flying Dick?"

"Gotta stake out your territory. Gay women know this. Straight women, you're totally clueless. You're trained to 'wait for the man.' Well, there's no man, in case you missed that. You're older, taller, and the one with the biggest hard-on, so take charge."

I gestured at her as if to say she was crazy. She shrugged and got up and headed back to her cabin.

"Hey, Jude." I imitated the song, and she turned around. "Thanks."

She gave me a little toast. "Good luck." And she sauntered off.

❖

It was late at night when the yearning became unbearable and I could no longer stay away from Levade. I told Sass if I was lucky, I wouldn't be back home tonight, so I was leaving him food and water, and a view of the lake from our bed. Then I walked through the trees along the lake and over to the Point and her cabin.

Levade was arguing with Tony, the same man she'd thrown out of her cabin before. Tony's shiny head and nearly featureless face, with his permanent squint and thin lips, made him look like a gray alien.

"You tell Frank he broke his promise, and that has consequences," she said. "He tried to rape her."

"Guess he forgot."

"Leave, and don't come back." The two shepherds were on him, and Levade never spoke their names but just gave them a hand signal to wait.

"Those two could have a bad accident," he said of the dogs.

"If that were to happen, I'd be standing graveside as they throw dirt on you."

He spat and walked off into the woods.

I stepped out of the shadows. "You want to tell me what that was all about?"

"He's a local guy who tries to act like a thug. Why are you here?"

"Why are you still so angry? I let Judith know it was a ridiculous thing, and nothing happened really, just so you know."

It was bad timing, because Levade was operating off a full head of steam from feuding with Tony.

"How fucked up are you?" she asked, and I was shocked. "You think sex with one lesbian will tell you if you like lesbian sex with me? Is a love relationship just mechanical for you? Why did I ever stir up Frank over you?

"What does that last thing mean?"

"Frank believes I'm attracted to you and that you make me happy, so of course he wants to put an end to that."

"Are you attracted to me?"

"You certainly don't make me happy!" she said, sounding so intensely angry that I was startled.

"Yet," I said forcefully, "I intend to rectify that situation." I walked up the cabin steps, pulled her inside with me, and locked the door. Then I took her hand and led her back to the airy bedroom with the linen drapes blowing in the wind, and a white, puffy, down coverlet.

"No. We can't do this," she said, looking surprised and worried.

"But we're going to," I said, and kissed her passionately, pressing her up against the wall so I could feel the full length of her, pulling her shirt aside to kiss her breasts. Her lips trailed my neck as my belly sought hers, and my pelvis rocked against her. The heat generated could have caused a cabin fire. I wasn't sure what I was doing exactly, but I knew what I wanted, and that desire seemed to drive everything. Wanting to be inside her was an overwhelming sensation.

"Slow down," she whispered. I kissed her again, while pulling her slacks off onto the floor as she unbuttoned my jeans. And then she propelled me onto the bed on top of her. It was the most exciting, erotic moment I'd ever experienced. I felt so light-headed I could have been deemed delirious.

"You are incredibly soft," she said.

"Is that a good thing?" I managed to breathe.

"A very good thing." Her eyes were shooting off sparks, and I knew at that moment that she possessed me. I breathed in hints of her exotic perfume on her hair and behind her ears, and my lips sought hers as I slid my fingers up her thigh and played at the edge of her desire, keeping her mouth locked to mine, connecting us like an electrical circuit, now so highly charged I thought we might simply short out. Then, unable to hold back any longer, I entered her suddenly, and she immediately thrust her hips into me, pushing her wet heat into my hand, open and throbbing, her intense, prolonged arousal having nearly brought me to climax. I held her as she clung to me, pounding against me, again and again, moaning her pleasure and then finally collapsing in a trembling, torrential release. I hoped her loneliness had been swept away in the tidal wave of her climax. And I waited only for that moment when I could entice her into climaxing again.

"Oh my God," I whispered. "That was so beautiful!"

She pushed me onto my back and kissed her way down my chest to my pubic hair, and then her face disappeared, and her hot mouth took all of me, her tongue pushing its way deeper and deeper inside me, then pulling away as if to demand that, if I wanted more, I would have to come to her, thrust myself into her, and I did, again and again, my hands entangled in her hair to keep her from leaving, from torturing me further.

I was nearly out of my mind in an orgasmic state I wanted to last forever. The tension, the rhythm, the sensation of her tongue in me disengaged my brain as I lunged into my own lust and erupted into a raging river. Then satiated, and silent, I lay exhausted, not knowing what had happened to me, the person who was never fully satisfied, the woman who could remain unemotionally attached.

Levade raised up on one arm to gaze into my eyes as her hand trailed over my breasts. She looked extremely pleased with herself.

"I suppose you think you've shown me who I am." I could barely whisper.

"I've only shown you who you are with me." And she was on top of me, putting her strong fingers inside me as I gasped and writhed and came in the intensity of her grasp.

❖

We made love all night, falling asleep just before dawn and then rising only to make love again. I was addicted to her. It was all I wanted to do—make love to her, be inside her, hold her, go down on her, be on top of her. It just made no logical sense for someone who wasn't new to sexual experiences. I wasn't hungry, or tired, just completely inexorably aroused by her. I ran my hands through her glorious hair and looked into her eyes, and she spoke softly. "Are you aware that I am in love with you?"

My heart stopped. I could never remember saying those words to anyone. The best I'd ever mustered was "Love you!" Saying a person's name, followed by 'I'm in love with you,' felt so committed. I pushed her back playfully, kissed her in lieu of response, and hopped up, saying, "I'm going to take a quick shower!" I needed to get away. I needed time to think.

This is the best I'd ever felt in my entire life. So why can't I just go with it...trust my instincts...trust her? Because it means making decisions, changes that might be irreversible. She is nothing short of the crossroads of my life.

I jumped out of the shower, toweled off, and put my jeans back on as she made coffee for me. I watched her move around the kitchen in her short, white, sexy nightshirt, with the collar up and the low-cut front. Every step she took, every gesture she made produced heat between my legs, and I deserted caffeine for her hot lips and beautiful naked body, pulling her back onto the bed, where I intended to stay forever. I was addicted to every part of her.

We were still in the bed when the knock came at the door, startling us both. I glanced at my watch. It was eleven o'clock in the morning.

Levade went to the door, and I was two steps behind her, feeling protective and wanting to communicate ownership.

Judith stood on the steps with flowers she'd obviously picked from the wildflower bed. She feigned surprise at seeing me. "There you are!" Like you didn't know, I thought. She probably watched my cabin all night to see if the lights ever came on, or if I came home. She most likely showed up this morning to entrap me.

She introduced herself to Levade and handed the flowers around the screen door to her. "For interrupting your morning. And don't you both look...rested." She turned her attention to me. "There's a guy who said he was asked to stop by and fix the screen on your lake pipe, Taylor. He's down by the dock. I told him I would fetch the famous author, which I'm sure would have impressed him if I thought he could read."

"I don't feel good about this. Don't go!" Levade warned me, but I was feeling pretty invincible after all those lovemaking sessions.

"The woman at the water department sent him. I'll point out the pipe and be right back. I promise." I gave her a searing look that said I expected to pick up where we'd left off.

I heard Judith echo reassuringly that I would be right back. "I'll keep Levade company until you return," she bubbled, and I thought, I bet you will.

I bounced down the hillside to the lake, feeling bonded to someone for the first time in my life. And I trusted Levade would not ever want anyone else. The arrogance of that assumption made me smile and actually skip for a couple of steps. *I didn't know I knew how to skip.* I laughed at myself.

Seeing no one on the dock, I walked west, down the shoreline, to my cabin, spotting a silver boat pulled up on the sand. He's in front of the wrong cabin, I thought. No wonder he can't find the lake pipe. The man waved to me as I walked toward him, and he had his tools with him. A few more strides and I stopped short, recognizing Tony.

Instantly, Tony stepped back into the underbrush as Frank grabbed me from behind, and I realized Tony was Frank's decoy. Frank clamped his iron hand over my mouth and forced me down into the boat. He tied my hands with the speed of someone roping a calf and blindfolded me, pushing me onto the seat opposite him.

"Sorry to interrupt your little liaison, but I didn't want you to get away without me showing you the deepest part of the lake," Frank said.

I screamed until I was nearly hoarse. Even my being blindfolded and seated in his boat in plain sight would appear normal to anyone watching from a distance. It would just appear to be Frank taking someone out for a tour to his secret fishing spots. I looked in what I thought was the direction of Levade's cabin, panicky and still screaming. How long would she wait before she looked for me? Frank revved the motor. I couldn't know if Levade was running in my direction, Judith behind her.

It dawned on me that Frank wanted her to see what he was doing. He wanted credit for it; he wanted her to be reminded that he could kill her, or anyone she loved. He wanted to control her.

Frank was so confident that he yelled his plans loudly over the sound of the motor. "I can tie you to the anchor and throw you overboard while I enjoy my lunch." He laughed and patted something on the boat bottom. "Then I'll hoist you up, cut the anchor rope, take off the blindfold, and people will find tragically that you couldn't swim very well."

Isn't anyone on the cove paying attention to this? Sound traveled, but was anyone listening? Frank threw the motor into full throttle, and the boat surged, throwing me violently forward onto the aluminum floor. My mind was racing so fast I thought I'd faint. Was he really intending to kill me or just terrorize me? He's a killer, my inner voice said. He kills.

"Frank, don't do this," I pleaded, shouting over the roar of the motor.

"What did you say? Can't hear you." He laughed.

It had only been a few minutes, but I was pretty sure we were far off the shoreline. Frank cut the motor and let the boat drift, beginning a psychotic dialogue into the wind.

"It's a shame about you. You're not the one who should die. I should kill Levade for fucking my wife, but if I killed her, I wouldn't have her to torture, so I'm going to kill what she loves, and too bad. Tag, you're it. You're her current happiness. She checks to see if I'm parked at your place, she checks to make sure you're home safe, she checks on you because she wants you—check, check, check—and I just can't let her have happiness, you know, after she took mine, after she made me kill my wife."

My mind raced back to Ben. He wasn't sick like Frank, but he had that same sense of everything in life being someone else's fault, and how he'd been done wrong, and therefore he had to make someone suffer for how unfair it all was. My fear of dying didn't diminish. I was terror-stricken, but on top of that fear was a layer of anger—anger at men who found women always at fault, anger at men who simply killed women when they disliked them, and anger over being about to die and not wanting to go down with a fucking whimper—and my anger was like kindling beginning to smolder and burst into flames.

"She had nothing to do with your wife's death. You killed your wife."

"She made me do it. If she hadn't been around—"

"You would have stopped beating her, bruising her, breaking her bones?"

"She made me do that!"

"No. You killed Dolores slowly for years by taking away her joy, controlling everything she said and everything she did. Even stuffing the little dogs she loved, so she had to look at them and mourn them every day. All Levade did was try to comfort her, because your wife was so fucking afraid of you, you sorry, sadistic sack of shit!"

"Keep talking, dead woman!" He slugged me, and I tasted my own blood, and I thought if I lived, I didn't want to be disfigured.

"But killing me won't keep you from experiencing what it feels like to be a disgusting, cowardly man—" He slugged me again, and my face hurt, and I wondered if he'd dislodged my teeth. "You can only hit women who are smaller, or weaker, or tied up and blindfolded." *Is this how it ends? I find the person who thrills me on the same day I find the one who kills me? The universe isn't even giving me twenty-four hours in between.*

He ripped the ties from my wrists and yanked the blindfold down to my neck, and while I was trying to get my bearings in the light, he swung the oar like a baseball bat, the flat side smashing my cheek. "There! Now we're on a level playing field."

The pain was excruciating. I thought about jumping overboard to escape him, now that I was untied, but I knew he would circle me with the boat, creating a vortex of water, and then run over me with the motor, cutting me to pieces. Staying in the boat seemed the only answer. *I have to put up a fight here.* I lunged at him. Unsteady and injured, I managed to grab him by the shirt front and hold onto him, wrestling with him as I pleaded, "You're her stepbrother. How could you do this to your sister?"

"She did it to me. She turned my father against me. She destroyed our family! She's a fucking lesbian cunt!" He shoved me backward and smashed his fist into me, and I remembered the dream of the woman who'd said "the wait is over" and I'd thought her words were warning me to stay out of the lake. Now I knew that I was right. It was simply over.

I couldn't tell if he was rocking the boat or if suddenly a breeze had picked up. Then I heard howling, the wind like an animal moving at warp speed, and dark clouds sweeping in out of nowhere. Whitecaps came up suddenly and threatened to wash over the side of the boat, and the winds felt cyclonic. Frank stumbled and lost his grip, and he obviously realized he had to get rid of me sooner than he'd planned.

"Little change in the itinerary," he said, and he swung the oar overhead, bringing it down like a hatchet. I threw my arms up to try to ward off the blow, but this time it felt like the edge had cut my skull in half.

In the fog of my injuries, I thought I saw a green metal boat trailing us, and then I was back at the cabin where the wind swooped the postcard off the desk and into the air, out the window, and up into the sky. I heard a woman's voice say, "Delivered," and I didn't know if she was talking about the postcard or my soul.

Then there was nothing, only blackness, and the pain was gone.

CHAPTER TWENTY-TWO

The pain was back, unimaginable pain, so much pain I wasn't sure where it was coming from. I struggled to open my eyes and squinted at the light above me. Everything was white, and I thought I must have died, and I wondered if I would see Angelique and Aunt Alice.

Then Levade leaned over me and kissed me gently on my forehead and face, and she had tears in her eyes. I heard her say, "She needs more pain medicine." And in the haze, rubber hands shot liquid into lines leading to IVs, and monitors tethered me like a large fish caught on a hook, and people hustled around me.

Judith and Levade were both standing at my bedside. I must have been in and out of consciousness, because I thought I heard Judith say, "It's us, all the women you've ever slept with."

Levade had my hand, and I squeezed her fingers and tried to smile.

I lost track of time. Outside my hospital room in the corridor, reporters gathered to find out what had happened. They'd heard a New York author was vacationing on the lake and had an accident.

Judith stepped out to greet them, and I heard her say she was a friend and an attorney staying in a nearby cabin. She could report that she and Levade were witness to Frank Tinnerson forcing me into his boat and taking me out into the lake. They followed to see what was going on, and a storm blew up.

"He hit Ms. James in the head with an oar and knocked her unconscious. When we came alongside, her assailant was nowhere to be seen. No photos or interviews until Ms. James is feeling well enough to get back to the new blockbuster novel she's writing."

"What were they fighting over?" a reporter asked."

Judith replied. "I don't know, but if he'd taken me against my will, I'd be fighting over that, wouldn't you?"

"Does she know Mr. Tinnerson?" another reporter asked.

"I think everyone in town will tell you they know Frank Tinnerson as the man who killed his wife."

Levade stepped back into my room, having to admit Judith did a good job, adding, "Judith gave a cute reporter her business card, saying, 'In case you need further information.'"

"Apparently lesbians move right along if we don't feel the love," I said, and Levade gave me a very sensual kiss.

"Do you feel the love?" she whispered.

"Could you do that again?" I whispered back.

Judith was witness to the kisses, and she peeked into the room, feigning irritation. "Could you two get a room...without monitors."

❖

Later, Ramona was on the phone with Levade. I don't know what day she called, or what hour, or if she asked for me and was told my attention span was still pretty short.

"No. I'm taking her home with me. I'll take care of her. Yes, give me your number," Levade said.

"I need your phone number," I parroted, and Levade smiled. "And I know what the *L* means..." I tried to draw a flourish in the air. "It means you love me," I said, and then I fell asleep again.

❖

Judith drove me home, while I sat cradled in Levade's arms in the backseat. They must have communicated with one another via looks and nods in the rearview mirror, because they said very little to me other than, "Are you in pain? Do you need a pain pill?"

Every bounce of the road caused me to emit a groan, and Judith apologized. People do that, I thought, in my foggy state. They apologize for driving you home over a bumpy road as if the road's condition is their fault. Like Levade apologizing for what her brother did to me. With any luck, he's dead anyway. Do I need to apologize for that?

The two of them hoisted me upright and dragged me up the porch steps, carrying me like one of those injured football players who leaves the field with a guy under each armpit like human crutches.

Marney had left dinner for Levade and Judith inside on the porch and a note saying she'd been checking on Judge Robertson for Judith. Thor and Helen brought a basket of fruit and some fresh berries from their store. It was touching that they'd made the drive just to deliver a homecoming gift. Casey delivered some magazines and a note that said, "Love conquers hate," but I wouldn't know any of this right away. I was focused on my two heads and how quickly I could get them to feel like one again.

Levade's bed was soft and reminiscent of the lovemaking we'd had there. She and Judith left me and talked in whispers out on the porch, while Sass curled up next to me and gently put his big head into my hand.

Finally Levade came back alone, Duke and Charlie trailing her. She'd been keeping them indoors with us, and I felt that until she knew for sure that Frank was dead, and not hiding somewhere in the woods waiting to finish me off, she wanted extra protection. Only Sass thought this wasn't such a great idea and eyed the two dogs constantly, probably monitoring their intentions.

"Can I get you anything?"

"Just your phenomenal body next to mine," I said, and she crawled into bed with me. Later she told me I slept ten hours without moving. I guess my body knew I was home.

The doctor phoned to check on me, which was so wonderfully small-town. He asked about headaches and dizziness and nausea and reminded Levade I would feel better in a week. I felt completely disconnected from the world other than hearing Levade talking to Ramona by phone. Levade tethered me to the earth. She was the one thing that made me happy.

It was unfair that our first weeks of living together, being together, were as patient and nurse. I knew it wasn't romantic for her to see me in the condition I was in, and despite my attempts at humor, I was often grumpy, to say the least. And then I had very strange thoughts. How do I not stay with Levade, who has loved me and nursed me back to health? I can't just say thank you and walk out the door. But if I stay in the way she wants me, would I be doing it because I feel obligated after what I put her through? And having seen me at my worst, why would she want me anyway? She's probably telling Judith right now that she doesn't want me. Maybe she feels obligated to stay with me because it was her stepbrother who tried to kill me. It must be the drugs.

❖

It was already late September; the air was crisp and the leaves were turning. It was the first day I could sit up and halfway think. Levade said she could tell I was getting better because I was cranky, demanding, and disobedient, which made me laugh.

"Was I ever obedient?" I asked. "Had I known I was, I would have stopped it immediately."

She'd put Sass on the bed with us, saying his vibes would calm me. Unfortunately, my vibes seemed to rub off on him instead, and he raked everything off the dresser and onto the floor and howled for hours.

"What does he want?" I pleaded over his howling.

"For you to get well. We all want that." She sounded sweet but tired. "They found Frank's body. He'd washed up alongside a beaver burrow in one of the coves across the lake. A knife was sticking in his heart."

"Oh, my God. Who stabbed him?"

"No one knows. Sam's outside, and he's asked if he can come in and talk to us."

I found it odd that Frank could kill his wife and no one investigated, but when Frank died trying to kill me, Sam wanted an investigation. But I said, "Sure. Bring him in."

Levade stepped out on the porch, and soon Sam entered, took off his hat, pulled up a chair, and sat down across from Levade and me.

"I don't want to take up too much of your time." He seemed self-conscious. "Levade told you they found a knife in Frank. Were you fighting him off with a knife?"

"Of course not. I got called down to the lake to talk to a repair guy, who turned out to be Tony, about the water pipe, and Frank jumped me. I had nothing on me. What kind of knife was it?"

"It was one Gladys said was missing from the hardware store—carved handle, a wolf peeking out of the trees."

"I remember it. I told her it looked like a work of art."

"Well, she thought maybe she misplaced it. She was sure it wasn't stolen because the case was locked. Knife had no prints of any kind on it."

"So what do you think, Sam?" Levade asked.

"I think in all the chaos and the storm, and the boat rocking, he may have fallen on it. Or the wind blew it into him."

I didn't think for a nanosecond that Sam believed that. It was a completely crazy theory. *How did Frank get the knife when Gladys never sold it to him? And how could a storm, short of a tornado, blow a knife into a man? And how would it just happen to land in his heart?*

"Is it possible that he washed up on shore, and someone put the knife in him after he was dead and couldn't fight back? Someone with enough anger to want to leave their mark in him? The list of people standing in line to do that would probably rival the number of suspects on the Orient Express," I said, the mystery writer in me coming out of the closet. "Or maybe," I said, "he lived through the storm."

"Frank was a good swimmer and a survivalist." Sam nodded. "Coroner says it's possible he could have been alive when he was stabbed."

"Then maybe as he tried to crawl out of the lake, someone else who had the knife, dove in, fought him, and killed him, and left him in the water, so there were no traces of blood on the shore. Of course that would take a pretty strong person with a pretty big grudge."

I thought about Little Man, who was at the hardware store looking at the knife Gladys was showing him. And how Gladys's daughter, Casey, had nearly been raped by Frank, and how Frank had killed Dolores, who might have had ties to Little Man. And then there was Kay, who had an affair with Dolores." But I didn't offer any more suspects or plot lines. I was pretty sure Sam already knew who did it, and so did Levade, and everyone involved felt justice had been served.

"Well, his death is officially a boating accident that occurred as a result of his attacking you, Taylor. That's what's in the report. You get well." He tipped his hat and left.

"What do you think?" I asked Levade.

"I think a lot of people killed Frank."

"He was still your stepbrother. Doesn't this make you sad?"

"No," she said in her straightforward, truth-telling style, and I sat quietly thinking about her lack of grief.

A small town that seemed to have given "Frank, who killed his wife" a pass, had left him to walk the streets, and brag about how he'd killed everything in the woods, and caught everything in the lake, had become an amorphous predator, biding its time and hiding in the bulrushes to bring him to justice.

CHAPTER TWENTY-THREE

I saw Judith this morning," Levade said in an upbeat tone that I'd come to learn was cover for her not feeling very upbeat. "She and her mother were packing up. She wished us well, and I got her contact information. She said it's a small world, and we might know some of the same people."

That made me smile. *Who are those people?*

"And here." Levade handed me a little piece of paper with her cell phone and cabin phone number on it, as if she knew I would soon need it, and for some reason it made me terribly sad. "You asked for it in the hospital. Do you remember?" I nodded that I did. "And in further news," her tone brightened, "the leaves are starting to turn, and the temperature has dropped. Fall is here."

I looked outside for the first time in a week, and the world had turned a rich gold, orange, and red. The leaves were glorious. The entire cove was awash in brilliant colors.

"I think that calls for lovemaking," I said, and she laughed out loud. "You find that request funny?"

"I don't think you're capable of it," she said sweetly.

"You'd be surprised what I'm capable of…but you have to cooperate." I held out my hand, asking her to come to bed. She lay beside me, and the moment her lips touched mine, my endorphins kicked in. "This has to be carefully choreographed," I warned her as she slid her hand between my legs.

"You mean like this?" she asked, and I immediately pulsed to her touch.

"Let me see if I understand," I murmured, and slid my fingers inside her. "Like this?"

She swooned and rocked into me, and me into her, and we kissed one another until we were simply our own pool of desire and moved in the same rhythm, like dancers in the night, and we climaxed simultaneously. I tried to catch my breath. "That's never happened to me before." I must have looked amazed.

"I would hope not," she said, and kissed me even more deeply, after which I fell asleep, not requiring a pain pill.

A few days later my curiosity had begun to return, a sure sign that I was getting better.

"You're psychic," I said. "You told me Frank would try to kill me."

"I knew he wouldn't succeed, but I had no idea he would hurt you like this. Particularly since I had proof he killed Dolores. She stopped by the drugstore and gave Casey a tape. Casey didn't have anyone she could trust, so one night she brought it to me."

I realized that must have been the night Casey came for a reading at Levade's cabin and then took something small from her pocket and gave it to her.

Levade seemed to be reading my mind, because she reached into a desk drawer and took out a tiny tape like the kind used in old answering machines. She put the tape into a dusty old recorder and punched play. A woman's voice said, "If I turn up dead, know that my husband, Frank Tinnerson, killed me. He told me he can shoot me any time he wants, and it'll be a hunting accident, because the men around here admire him."

It was surreal to hear the voice of a dead woman whose fears had come to pass.

"I went to Pine City to clear out my mother's home and take care of what little business she had. Frank wanted some of her things related to his father," Levade said. "I arranged for us to go at separate times, and I had a neighbor meet him.

"Frank insisted we meet at the coffee shop afterward. That's where I told him I had the tape, and if he didn't leave you and me alone, I'd turn it over to the authorities. He sent Tony to ransack my cabin looking for it, but I came home and caught him. Since Tony found nothing, Frank no longer believed the tape existed, so he felt free to come after you to punish me."

"And when I went down to the lake and left you with Judith?"

"I heard you screaming. Or if I didn't actually hear you, I heard you in my head. I knew you were in trouble, and we followed immediately. Judith called Sam, and fortunately he was on the lake in his speedboat. We got to you about the same time. He radioed ahead, and an ambulance met us on shore in about fifteen minutes. You'd fought so hard to stay alive, and I was terrified I'd lost you, because you were bleeding so badly."

Levade wrapped herself around me as if talking about the nightmare made her relive it. I hugged her close, loving her even more...more than anyone I'd ever known.

"I'm sorry I scared you." I kissed her, and then to avoid tearing up, I focused on the facts. "So you, me, and Judith all rode to shore in Sam's speedboat."

"Yes. Once you were in the ambulance, Sam went back out on the lake to get the duck boat to shore. Of course, I didn't care about the boat. I only cared about you."

I kissed her warm lips and cuddled her close to me.

"I begged Angelique to save you, and she must have kept your head above water to keep you from drowning, because you were unconscious when we pulled you out," Levade whispered.

"Do you think Angelique killed Frank?"

"The storm, the town, Angelique, we all killed Frank." She said nothing more, and I dropped the subject.

Levade's cell phone buzzed. Ramona was on the line asking about my condition, and Levade put me on the phone.

"Are you well enough to come back to New York and do some book signings for your last release, and we can tease your upcoming one? The press has gotten wind of this whole attack by Frank, and they're thrilled by the near-murder of the murder-mystery author. I swear people get off on the damndest things, but hey, I'll take it."

"I'm doing just fine, thanks, and happy to supply you with a promotional hook, albeit my near-death." I rolled my eyes at Levade.

"Great. I can book a plane for you, if you could get here this week. A lot going on."

"Okay. I'll get back to you right away." I hung up, not wanting to say more in front of Levade.

"She wants you back in New York." Levade turned away. "What does all this mean for us?"

"I…we…can't stay here in winter, anyway. Are you really intending to stay?"

"I live here…mostly."

I fretted because I knew we were at the juncture other women had traveled with Levade—wanting her to be someone else, move somewhere else.

"The ice on the lake freezes eight feet thick. You can drive a truck across it. Maybe we should wait and come back next year. We could go to New York together, eat in nice restaurants, see a few shows, and you could come to the book signings. We'll freeze here, and there's nothing to do really."

"Nothing but write, read, heal, and make love." She smiled. When I didn't respond, she pressed the issue. "Are we making love, or are we in love?" She spoke to me quietly, and I knew a land mine awaited this answer. She was calling me out for my non-response in bed when she'd told me she was in love with me.

"We're…together." I couldn't express what I felt, how much I loved and adored her, what she meant to me, and yet, I couldn't stay. Staying meant an end to…well, to however my life was. It felt like the death of something. Why had I spent all those years in school and struggling in New York, and honing my craft, and making contacts in the city, if I was going to throw it all away for someone, and then that someone might not like me after a while? I'd been told often enough by lovers that I didn't "wear well."

"Just 'together'?"

"More than together." I tried to course-correct.

"For a moment you almost said what you wanted."

"I want you," I said.

"I can't live in New York."

"Be here next spring, wait for me," I pleaded.

"Next spring?" She spat the words and looked at me with anger and hurt and disappointment, as if "next spring" had just relegated her to a summer fling. Why did I think I could be without her until spring, and I searched for words to apologize, but she spoke first.

"I don't wait, Taylor," she said, and she walked out.

Levade didn't come back. I slowly gathered up the clothes she'd brought me from my place, but I finally gave that up. Just the act of moving around the cabin, without her here, was so sad I couldn't stay another minute. Her energy was so big and pure and loving that her physical absence seemed to suck all the joy out of the place, and I wanted to run. I made it back to my cabin in tears and packed. Then I sat on the porch with the moonlight flooding the lake and drank a glass of wine. I'd forgotten I'd taken a pain pill but decided if the combination killed me, this would be the perfect time.

I fell asleep in the chair and awoke at two in the morning and hobbled off to bed. I dreamed that Angelique appeared, or maybe she actually did—the pill and the alcohol made that hard to determine. She pulled up a chair beside my bed and said,

"Rejecting a cosmic gift isn't good." I woke up sad and disturbed by the dream. *What do you mean "isn't good"? Not good as in I'll be struck by lightning, never see her again, die forlorn? Jesus!*

❖

Marney came over at dawn and told me how wonderful it had been to have me here, and how she prayed for me to get well, and how she hated to see me go. "Come back next summer. I'll be sure not to book the Robertsons during the weeks you're here."

"The Robertsons are fine. Nice people," I said, and she looked confused.

"It's the woman on the Point, isn't it? It's Levade. You two have gotten very close, I can tell. And I don't think we gave her a fair chance. She's not crazy, or you wouldn't be so crazy about her. You could stay a little longer, you know. We're a couple of months from serious weather."

"Thanks, Marney," I gave her a long, genuine hug. "But I have to go."

"To what?" she said, wiping her eyes as she headed out that door. "Sometimes people don't even know why they're coming or going—they just keep moving."

Marney was smarter than I gave her credit for. In fact, she was a lot smarter than me.

I loaded the car and locked the cabin. Levade was standing beside her Jeep when I went out to get in my SUV. I threw myself at her, hugging her despite all the body pain I still felt.

"I was going to drive over to your cabin to say good-bye. What can I do to get you to—"

She kissed me.

"We'll see each other again, Taylor. You're meant to be mine. Angelique saved you for me, and actually you've saved me." Her expression was serious, as if she wanted to say more, but instead, she got in her Jeep and drove away, never looking back.

I thought my heart would break. I sat slumped over the wheel miserable and already lonely. Finally, I pulled myself together, backed out of the drive, and headed down the road, saying good-bye to the majestic pines and the sparkling lakes and loving Levade.

What the fuck was I doing getting involved with her? *And what the fuck am I doing leaving her and the damned cat?* I dehumanized Sass to avoid the pain of losing him too. *And why am I leaving Muskie Lake, in danger of drowning in my own tears?*

CHAPTER TWENTY-FOUR

I rang Levade from the Minneapolis airport, and she picked up the cabin phone immediately.

"I made a mistake," I said quietly. "Already I can't stand to be away from you."

"I miss you so much," she said. "I wish you could have stayed."

"I want to turn around and come back, but now I'm obligated in New York because Ramona has set up a promotional —"

"There are no mistakes, Taylor. We are all doing exactly what we're supposed to be doing in this moment. I love you."

"My plane is boarding," I said.

"Go," she said sweetly, and she hung up. I ran to catch the plane, slung my duffel into the overhead bin, and slouched in my first-class seat, unable to hold back the tears that flooded my eyes and rolled down my cheeks and onto my shirt. I took out a mirror to fix my makeup and realized I looked like I'd been on a three-day drunk, so I put on my sunglasses and assumed people would think I was in mourning, which in fact I was.

By the time I landed, my head hurt from the air pressure in the plane, reminding me that I had residual pain from what I'd been through, but my head was nothing compared to the pain in my heart.

I rang Levade again to tell her I had arrived in one piece, and she picked up the cabin phone. Standing in the chaos of LaGuardia,

I could barely hear her. She said she knew I would be safe, and she was happy for me regarding my book.

"I just wish you were with me," I said.

"Taylor, you have things to do, and things to understand about yourself. It will be easier if you focus on that now and not on me. I love you so much." She hung up, clearly no longer expecting "I love you" in return.

That night I rang her from my apartment that now looked completely alien to me, as if I'd never lived here, as if I were no longer the person who slept in that wrought-iron bed, or stared up at the tall, dusty bookcases, or out at the traffic through the wall of windows. I had no nostalgia for any of the apartment's kitschiness, no connection to its being my home, and no desire to stay here.

Levade didn't answer. I called her from taxi cabs and lunch counters and my bed late at night. I called multiple times every day, ringing her cabin phone, then her cell phone. I got nothing. And it stayed that way. She never answered again. In desperation, I called Helen at Muskie Market and Marney in the white cabin, and they both said she was still there. I was relieved that nothing had happened to her, but distraught beyond words that she was blocking me out of her life.

❖

The book signing was for my last novel, *Twelve O'clock*, and an excuse to tease my upcoming release. It took place in It's Only Words, a large, popular bookstore in Soho. I smiled, thanked each person who stood in line to praise my work, then requested a name. "Mandy. M-A-N-D-Y?" I confirmed the spelling and then wrote, "Mandy, the time is now! Enjoy the read." I signed the book Taylor, then handed it to her.

I was working numb, on autopilot, not from feeling so little, but from feeling so much. I'd cried so long over Levade that I was physically and emotionally spent. We'd had those two phone conversations on the day I flew back to New York, and then, over the past two weeks, she'd stopped answering the phone altogether. I left messages, but she never returned my calls. I teared up thinking about that, and thus the punk sunglasses to hide my bloodhound eyes and make me appear cool rather than heartbroken. Beyond that, I just smiled and signed.

After six hours, the book signing ended, and the last book I signed was for Kay in Muskie, the bartender who had an affair with Frank's wife. I decided to send it to her on a whim, thinking maybe she'd enjoy it. The bookstore manager, glad the event had gone well, offered to mail it to her. I wrote, "Kay, love will find you. Taylor."

Several reporters had come in late and wanted to interview me about what happened on Muskie Lake. One young reporter aggressively intercepted me.

"Ms. James, I wanted to find out firsthand what happened to you in Minnesota. Local papers said you were attacked by a man who tried to kill you." He was obviously new at his job, because his question contained the answer, so I tortured him for that mistake.

"Yes," I said.

"Yes, you were attacked?"

"Yes," I replied.

An older, more experienced female reporter jumped in. "Can you describe the experience for us, and why you think it happened?"

"The man was deranged. He had given me a guided tour of the lake, and that's the context in which I knew him. He ambushed me and kidnapped me and tried to beat me to death in his boat and nearly succeeded. Coming that close to death makes you determined to live life more fully. Thanks for your time." I walked away, directly into Ben, who was standing there waiting for me, as the female reporter shouted a follow-up question. "How do you intend to live more fully?" I ignored her. That was for me, not the entire world, to know.

I focused on Ben. My old reaction, adrenaline shooting through my body and creating a desire to run, had evaporated; nonetheless just seeing his face in such close proximity increased my heart rate. *You're in a public place and you're mentally stronger than he is now. Relax.*

He looked like an older, chubbier meme of himself, wearing a three-piece suit and a big grin.

"So, the famous author returns. Just came by to say congratulations and ask if I could buy you dinner. I've had a few years to think about this, and I've decided you and I were the best together."

"I've had years to think about it too, Ben. You were a dumbfuck." I said the words, remembering how Levade had shocked me when she used that particular expletive on the dipshit deputies at the sheriff's office. "I put up with you, Ben, which speaks to how disempowered I was. But I've changed, and this much I know—I don't want to have a relationship with you, or anyone like you." Fatigue had enabled me to speak in a calm, disinterested manner. *Something to be said for lack of sleep.*

"So sounds like you're all cocky because you think you're somebody."

"Yes, I am somebody. Everybody's somebody," I said wearily, recognizing the old pattern, the way he used to build to a raging fight, beginning with him attacking who I thought I was and ending with a barrage of reminders about how I was nothing...nothing without him and his money and his contacts. A knot started gathering in my neck, and I moved my head around to try to loosen it.

"So you're seeing someone, obviously."

"I'm seeing everyone. In fact, I'm seeing myself for who I am. I'm the woman who put up with your insecure, vicious, abusive, sorry, sack-of-shit behavior." I was aware I was repeating words I'd shouted at Frank, and somehow it felt appropriate. I turned suddenly and took a step forward, invading his personal space.

"And just so you know, Ben, the last man who tried to destroy me was found dead in a lake with a knife in his chest."

I walked past him and heard him say, "Medication, seriously!" His nervous tone made me smile.

Ramona appeared, gave me a hug, and offered to buy me a drink next door, at a quaint little pub, rescuing me from further conversation with Ben.

The pub was so dark it acted as sunglasses, so I took mine off and hooked them in my shirtfront.

"Seems like it went well. Big crowd. Lots of good comments." She spotted a private corner and headed in that direction. "Wish you were as bright-eyed as the color of that suit. What is that color?" She feigned ignorance.

"Gold is the new black," I said.

"Only if you're Aretha Franklin."

We slung our bodies into the lounge chairs and ordered a drink. "Good coverage in the *Times*. Great anticipation for your upcoming lesbian mystery-romance." Ramona rolled her eyes. "A genre I had to create since I'd pitched a hard-core murder-mystery. Anyway, they think it will be an interesting departure from your past work, greatly anticipated, yada yada. Did you read the article?"

"I don't read the press comments. Even when you think the review is nice, I always consider it marginal."

"Listen to this." She pulled two clippings out of her bag. "'Mystery writer bringing home a real-life murder mystery.'" And "'Taylor James back in our lives—'"

"Levade isn't talking to me anymore. The landline reception sucks, and now she's not answering it anyway. I don't understand why she won't talk to me."

"I bust my balls to get you great press, and you are incredibly ungrateful." Ramona's outburst was unlike her. It was clear I was trying her patience.

"I'm sorry. Thank you, for everything you do." I felt tears gathering. *All I fucking do is cry!* "I sent you a sneak peek of the new manuscript. It's in your email. You should read your email occasionally."

Her eyes widened in apparent surprise. I took the cabin key out of my pocket and pushed it across the table in her direction. "You see, it wasn't all for nothing. Thank you."

There was silence between us, during which I sipped my wine, and Ramona belted down a vodka martini. I panned the room, checking out the pretty women and important-looking men, all of whom were meeting and greeting and socializing, and I felt completely disconnected—as if I were an extra in a big motion picture and had been told to appear to be interested, but not too interested.

I snapped back when Ramona moaned, "Go there when the tour is over, in the spring when it starts to get warmer. You can't use the cabin now anyway. It's not winterized."

"I have never felt this way about anyone. What's wrong with me. I can't stand it!" My voice was shaky.

Ramona let out a long sigh, "You're in love for the first time in your life."

I stared at her. "Is this how bad being in love feels?"

"In your case, apparently. It might have a late-in-life intensity."

"What if she finds someone else?"

"Oh, for God's sake." Ramona seemed to fret about what to say next and finally uttered, "Marney's red cabin is winterized. Just do the five book signings, the press interview, and then go."

"You'll call Marney?"

"She's got Sam on standby. She thinks it's 'Oh, for sweet' that you're in love."

I grabbed her and hugged her close.

"Easy," she said. "Marney tells me this lesbian thing can 'rub off' on people."

"You should be so lucky." I winked at her.

I was happy again, with renewed purpose—seeing Levade. I continued to call her cell and the cabin, but she didn't answer. I got phone numbers for Sam at the sheriff's office, and Gladys at the hardware store, and anyone else I could think of to ask about her. No matter who I talked to, I felt they knew more than they were saying, and they were basically saying nothing. Levade might be odd, but she was theirs, and I was just another summer tourist. When it came down to it, the town might gossip about one another, but they never gave up one of their own.

So I counted the days between book signings, and the hours between press interviews, and I was once again the bubbly, cooperative author Ramona had hoped "summer at the cabin" would resurrect.

❖

When the last PR event was over in November, I headed for the airport. As I was waiting to board, I glanced over at the gift shop and spotted a ceramic salt-and-pepper shaker of a giant ape kissing the Empire State Building. Marney, I thought. I ran over and told the clerk I would take it. She raised an eyebrow, and I knew she was questioning my taste.

"It's a gift," I said, then realized that explanation made it sound worse.

"Forty-five dollars," she said.

"For this cheesy little tchotchke?"

She turned the Empire State Building upside down, and salt poured out. She tilted the gorilla, and pepper came out of his penis. "And a lovely gift for that special someone." She smirked.

I love New Yorkers, I thought, and forked over the forty-five bucks. Then I dashed to catch my plane to Minneapolis, all bundled up and flying in bumpy weather to the Northwoods, with King Kong and his pepper dong in my pocket.

Normally, flying anywhere in bad weather, I would fear for my life, but having Frank nearly kill me, and then knowing Levade could be waiting for me, I was unafraid, even when I had to take a puddle jumper the last two hundred miles because the roads were bad.

I landed at the tiny airport outside Muskie and rented one of two sedans available, not the best vehicle for snowy roads, but it was all they had. I found Ramona's lip liner in the seat. This was the car she'd driven to come to the cabin, and no one had used it since. I tucked her makeup into my jacket pocket to take to her.

My drive to the woods was cold, twenty-four degrees, with six inches of snow on the ground. Winter had just begun. I skipped cabin #1 and went to #3, the red cabin. The lake was gray and foreboding, the cabins like a ghost town. I lifted the frozen-stiff doormat as Marney had instructed and found the key underneath it, along with a note from Sam, who was caretaking.

Welcome! Heat and electric are on. Dock's been pulled for winter, so don't use the lake.

I'd forgotten that the long boat docks are put in the lake each summer by men in waders wielding sledgehammers, who pound the posts into the clay and sand, and then nail the dock on top. Winter ice would push the posts over, so docks are removed in late fall. The shoreline looked nude without them.

No one was around, which was a bit frightening for a city person. No light on at the Point or any sign of inhabitants. Even Marney and Ralph had taken a few months off.

I tossed my luggage onto the bed, selecting the larger bedroom in order to forget the tryst with Judith in the smaller one. I turned on the lights and the heat, which was more modern than in Ramona's cabin, boasting an electric thermostat on the wall. If they could modernize the heating, why couldn't someone tackle the hideous decor? Then I set the pair of gorilla salt-and-pepper shakers in the center of the dining-room table. *Probably the most interesting item this cabin has ever seen, with the exception of the flying dildo.*

I'd brought a few essentials to get me through until stores were open, so I brewed a pot of coffee, sat down in a rocker, and stared at the bleak landscape—all the golden colors gone, the crystal-clear lake now gray, reflecting the sky, and ice coating the limbs of every tree where leaves used to be.

Ramona rang the cabin phone to make sure I'd arrived and that Marney had arranged for a key. The sound told me the phone lines were working, so clearly Levade had ignored my calls.

"Is she there?"

"The place looks boarded up," I said.

"So what's your plan?"

"I just have to find her."

"You can't sit there like a mother bird on a dead egg. She might not be coming back. You need a better plan than sit and wait."

"You're just making me crazier. Do you mind? Give me a day or two to figure this out."

"Taylor, did you ever consider that this might have been a summer fling for her? After all, she's not the crazy psychic with the white horse everybody thought she was. She obviously has a life beyond the lake. And how would it work for the two of you, I mean, after you find her? Do you live up there in the woods and write? It sounds wonderful, the idea of having a dog, feeding the chipmunks, watching the fish jump—but look out the window, sweetie. It's *Fargo*. It's *Frozen*. 'Winter is coming!' It's so cold your tits fall off!"

"I'll call you later," I said and hung up. The sound of my own voice had been oddly comforting, and now I was alone in the silence.

CHAPTER TWENTY-FIVE

At dawn, I dressed in ski pants and a parka, then drove out to the Point. From the road, the property gates were locked, a clear sign she was gone. I couldn't drive my car any farther, so I got out and walked to the cabin, peering in windows and then banging on the door. I don't know what I was looking for, but it was clear Levade wasn't there. I even looked around for recent dog manure, thinking if she'd been here a couple of days ago, maybe Charlie and Duke would have left a sign, but then I quickly reminded myself the dogs would be back home with Sam, and he could have brought them out here with him to check on the property. Either way, it didn't matter. The snow-covered ground was pristine.

In town at Muskie Market, Helen and Thor greeted me warmly. I no longer made a secret of the fact that I desperately wanted to find Levade, and I was pretty sure they understood that we were more than friends, but I no longer cared.

"Well, ya, she left about two weeks ago or more. She waited longer than normal, but weather coming up, she had to go," Helen said. "How're you feeling after...what happened."

"Better every day," I said. Then I stopped myself. "Actually, I'd be doing a lot better if I could find Levade. Do you have any idea where she might have gone?"

"Not my business," Thor said jovially, as if suggesting it shouldn't be mine.

"I called, but she never answered."

"Ya, phone lines went down for, what, Helen, a week or ten days, and, a course, cell-phone service isn't working much." Helen confirmed his reporting.

I felt better that maybe Levade wasn't avoiding me but just didn't get my calls. *But then why didn't she drive into Pine City, where they have better service? And why would she knock herself out to call me? I'm the one who walked off and told her to sit like a house plant till spring.*

I bought a few groceries and loaded them in the car, which was as cold as a refrigerator. Then I walked into Gus's tavern, glad he'd taken a break and Kay was there alone, taking care of two or three patrons. I was the only person seated at the bar.

"You'll find her," she said without me even asking the question. "How you doing?"

"Better physically. Miserable mentally."

"Well, when you find what you need, don't give up on it."

I thanked her, fighting back tears.

"Hey, Tony, the bald guy, he pulled up stake and left town. Wanted to let you know in case you were thinking of using him for odd jobs." But I knew she was telling me about Tony simply to say he'd been swept out of my life after setting me up to be killed.

She shifted gears. "I got your book, *Twelve O'clock.* I'll read it, you betcha. Hey, you missed my birthday."

"No kidding. Well, happy birthday!"

"I'm a Virgo. Things have to be buttoned up. I got some really nice gifts. Snowshoes, your mystery novel for when I'm socked in this winter, and a friend gave me a really neat knife." Her eyes locked with mine. "Best gift I ever got."

I stared at her for a long moment.

"Well, gotta get to work." She ignored me after that, hailing a couple she knew who came through the door. I tossed money onto the counter for my Coke and left.

I wondered how many people in town knew that Kay had an affair with Frank's wife, and that Kay was probably the last person to see Frank alive. If they all knew it, I doubted it would become her descriptor. And who's the friend who gave her the knife? Did Little Man talk to Gladys, and she slipped it to him, and he gave it to Kay? Or did Casey open the locked display case in her parents' hardware store and remove the knife, giving it to Kay to repay her for having hauled Frank off her?

The place where Frank washed up on shore was closest to Kay's cabin, and she's a good-sized woman who did a stint in the navy, but if she did kill him, how would she know exactly when he was out there in the lake, either swimming for his life or dead off her shoreline. Only Sam in his sheriff's boat, with the searchlights and sonar, could have spotted Frank's body in the water in time to let anyone know. I paused to think about that. Did Sam radio Kay to be on the lookout for Frank? Would Sam do anything to keep his promise to Angelique and protect Levade?

I headed down Main Street to the café and the hardware store, asking about Levade in each place, but the answer was the same. *By nightfall they'll all have talked to one another about my searching for Levade.*

Last stop was the drugstore for aspirin. Casey was working the place alone, since all the tourists were now gone. Only the hard-core hunters and ice fishermen were in town, dead and bloodied deer strapped to the roof racks of their cars, as if to let the carcasses speak for their manliness.

Casey seemed glad to see me and shouted, "Hey, Ms. James. You're looking for Levade, aren't you?"

"Do you know where she is?"

"No. But I'm glad you're here, because something's been bothering me. I wanted to tell you that I lied to you that time about going out to the Point to get a reading from her. It was me you saw."

I nodded and waited for her to get the courage to tell me why she lied. "Frank's wife used to come in for ice cream, and we'd talk a little. After she and Kay stopped Frank from, you know, hurting me, I guess he took it out on her and she got scared, and she told me that if she was ever found dead, I should know Frank did it. She gave me a tape, but I never let the sheriff know, and I'm so sorry I didn't. I wished I could go back and do it over again. I went to Levade, hoping she could tell that to Dolores, you know, on the other side. Tell her I was sorry."

"I'm sure she got the message to her," I said.

"She did. Made me feel better."

"So when they found Frank, he had a knife in his chest," I said casually.

"Yeah. No one can figure how that knife got out of the case over at the hardware store. No prints or nothin'. Maybe Dolores did it," she gave me a quirky grin, "you know, to make him pay for what he did." And I remembered Levade saying that's what Kay wanted, for Frank to 'pay for what he did.' Casey rang up my purchases, telling me to watch the fog that moves in off the lakes. "It can blind you, and you can end up in a quicksand bog."

She was right. The drive to the cabin was nerve-wrecking, the headlights unable to penetrate the curtain of white mist that billowed off the lakes and across the forest ground, and shifted into images that disintegrated and then re-formed right before my eyes. It was both dangerous and spooky, and I thought I saw Angelique walking ahead of me down the road. Even though I felt I knew Angelique, seeing a slightly disembodied ectoplasmic version of her walking ahead of my moving vehicle was enough to creep me out, so I shouted at her to regain some sense of control. "Angelique, help me find her, damn it!" It was crazy, my shouting into the fog, but it seemed to help me shake the fear. "And, if you held my head above water during the storm, then you saved me, and thank you, and I hope you saved me for Levade." The billowing image faded into the mist.

I was grateful to reach the cabin, where I unloaded my groceries and built a fire in the fireplace. Actually, I just set a match to the wood and kindling already there, prepared by Sam for people like me who failed to earn their Fire Builder Girl Scout badge.

Then, I sat in a chair that let me see Levade's cabin from mine, wishing with all my heart that a light would suddenly come on and I could run to meet her, and crawl into bed with her, and hold her close to me.

I waited, comforted by being where Levade once was. Suddenly Ben crossed my mind. My God, what in the world made me stay with him? Maybe it was the feeling that I didn't deserve better, or maybe I felt I'd gotten exactly what I deserved. What I want is Levade, I thought. I deserve that kind of happiness. I thought about her touch, her laugh, her beauty, her kind heart, and how I wanted her…only her, forever, and how I'd rejected her when she told me she wanted that for us…and I broke down and sobbed.

I fell asleep in the chair and dreamed that a dark-haired woman rose out of the lake and told me to follow the white horse. I awoke abruptly, startled, and said out loud, "Where is the white horse? Where is her white horse? She had to send him somewhere, and not every place takes horses."

❖

At daybreak, I phoned Sam, and he met me at the sheriff's office, where he had his feet up on the desk reading a newspaper.

"What's got you up at dawn? Things are just so exciting here that you missed us all?"

"I did miss you! Sam, where did she take her horse? How do you contact her?"

"She's a private person, Taylor. She wouldn't like me sharing any information with anyone." *He knows. He knows!*

I lunged over the metal desk and yelled, "Damn it, Sam! Tell me where she is! I love her! I'm IN love with her. I want to be with her!" I could see from his expression that the words shocked him, and in fact, they shocked me. I had finally said I was in love with someone, a woman, and out-loud, and to Sam. And Levade's words filled my head. "Until you say it, you can't have it."

Sam stared at me for what seemed like a long time, then pulled open the metal desk drawer and took out a pencil and spoke as he scribbled something on a scrap of paper. "I helped your aunt Alice and Angelique, so I guess I can help you." He handed over an address in Illinois and a phone number.

"Thanks, Sam. I love you too!" I kissed him on the cheek, and he reddened, though he smiled.

I hopped into the car and raced back to the cabin, stuffed my clothes into a bag, locked up the place, and left. I called the airline along the way. There would be one flight out today to Illinois, if I could get to Minneapolis by ten thirty a.m., and I thought, I'll get there if I have to rent a plane.

When I returned the rental car, the man sitting in a booth the size of an outhouse peeked out of the door and said, "You just got here. That didn't seem like much of a vacation."

I told him it had turned out to be perfect. "A cup of coffee, a view of the lake, a good night's sleep, and thank you." I handed him the keys and some cash, since he didn't accept credit cards.

"Well," he shook his head, "I hope no one else feels that's all they need, or I'll be outta business." *The guy thinks he's in business with two rental cars.* I smiled at him. *I guess maybe he is.*

I drove two hours to the iron-mining town of Hibbing and caught a flight to Minneapolis that put me on the tarmac at ten a.m. There, I ran to the terminal to board a ten thirty a.m. flight for Chicago, slumping into my seat just as the doors were closing. In between, I called the number Sam had given me but got a recording. It was a horse facility, but the answering machine said they were currently out of the office.

The plane ride to Illinois was harrowing. The nice middle-aged woman in the window seat next to me clutched her rosary and fretted, saying we could die in this weather.

"This is going to be a very nice flight," I said, repeating what Angelique had told me on my flight north, and that made me laugh. *Are you here?* I mentally spoke to Angelique and wished she were.

"How do you know this will be a nice flight?" The woman twisted in her seat.

"Because I know the angels who protected me all summer didn't do it merely to toss me out of this plane before I get to be with the love of my life," I said cheerily.

"My husband, the love of my life, ran off with another man last week! How do you like that?"

My brain scanned an entire list of potential responses before I landed on, "Life's full of changes."

"Changes, yes. Sodomy, no!" She recoiled, plastering her face so tightly against the window she looked like an anti-bird-collision sticker.

I put on headsets to prevent further conversation and listened to Taylor Dayne sing "Love Will Lead You Back." Whether it was the lady on the plane or old Minnow-Munching-Maynard, people suffered when love left. I knew that feeling, and I was determined it wasn't going to happen to me again.

I checked my watch every five minutes, willing the plane to go faster, and finally the wheels touched down. It was one p.m., I'd made it to Illinois, and I felt like I'd been awake for three days. I'd never traveled so far, so fast, and to so many places just on chance. If I stopped to think about it, my trip to the Northwoods, because Levade didn't answer my calls, was insane. And now, here I was, in Illinois, based on Sam's scribbled address, and having no idea if Levade was even here. *I accused Levade of strange behavior. I'm practically certifiable.*

CHAPTER TWENTY-SIX

It was cold but sunny when I checked the address above the gate. The huge iron posts stood about fifteen feet in the air and held an elaborate locked gate with elegant ironwork that read LIPIZZANER FARMS: THE WINTER HOME OF THE LIPIZZANER STALLIONS. The *L* had that same flourish Aunt Alice made on her postcard. I stood there for a moment taking that in. Aunt Alice obviously knew this place and how Angelique loved it, and she took that swooping *L* on the gates of this fabulous farm and made it her code for "I love you" in a time when lesbians couldn't simply say those words to one another out loud. I knew the *L* was a sign that I was in the right place, not just geographically, but in my soul.

I punched gate buttons and the visitor voice box, but no one responded, so I parked the rental car off to the side of the massive drive and decided to walk in. I took off my parka and held my breath so I could squeeze between two iron bars in a row of metal that was their farm fence, and then I quickly put my down jacket back on.

It was a long, cold walk to the barn, but I was thrilled to finally be here. Ahead of me were three long, white-and-gray stone barns, with very tall ceilings and high windows, and the heads of white horses sticking out of them. In a field to one side, a few horses were out for exercise. *What if she's with someone else? What if she isn't excited to see me? What if...what if...what if?* I marched in cadence to my fretting as I reached the closest barn in this wonderland of white horses.

I entered, looking for someone I might tell of my arrival. No one answered my "Helloooo!" so I continued to look around. The horse stalls were large and pristine, magnificent in their gold embellishments, and they ran endlessly in one long row on the window side of the aisle, while the opposing wall was a visual catalogue of the long history of the facility, with murals and huge photos of famous horses and horsemen.

Suddenly, a nicker, and I looked behind me. The name plate said ALIZAR and, below his name, his lineage as son of yet another Alizar.

I dashed over to his stall, delighted to see him, and he seemed to remember me. I gave him a pat and a cheek kiss.

"With what I know now, Alizar, I have a feeling your daddy may have been named in honor of my aunt Alice, Alice Armand. Alice-Ar. Alizar." He put his head down to allow me to rub him. "Where is she? Where's Levade?" But the elegant horse was giving up no secrets. "Tell you what. I'm staying with you, because I know wherever you are, she will be, at least by dinnertime."

❖

Twilight and the sun angled through the high windows and cascaded down into the aisle, making the view beyond a few yards blinding. I almost felt Angelique was there. Suddenly, Levade appeared in the aisle in her riding clothes and paddock boots, looking phenomenal.

"Taylor?" She seemed to know instinctively I was there.

"That is a very hot outfit. You look gorgeous."

She froze. "What are you doing here?" she whispered, and I could hear her take a breath.

I walked the distance to her as if approaching a shrine, and I kissed her like I never knew I could kiss anyone, and she collapsed in my arms. "I came to be with you."

"I stay here with Alizar in the winter, and I go back to the Point in the spring." She began with our geography problem.

"Me too."

"I don't go to New York," she warned me, a bit breathless.

"Where you go, I go." I stopped and took a breath. "Levade, I'm in love with you. I am madly, irrationally, in love with you. I want to be with you forever." I'd finally said it, and the look in her eyes melted me. I kissed her as if we were alone and no one would ever see how much I wanted her. I kissed until we were both a river of longing.

"You'll stay here with me in my apartment. Wait right here and I'll—"

"I don't wait," I said and grabbed her around the waist and walked with her. "I brought you something." I produced a jump drive from the pocket of my parka. "It's the first draft of my manuscript entitled *White Horse Point*. I wrote it about…well, I wrote it because of you." And she tucked it into her riding vest and hugged me.

We walked through the massive stone training barn, down the long horse aisles, large pictures of famous trainers and equestrians lining the walls. I stopped abruptly in front of a huge photograph of a tall woman in riding clothes, her hair slicked back, making her look extraordinarily dashing. Standing next to her were several magnificent white horses.

"Angelique!"

"Yes. This was the place she loved. She only went to the Point to be with your aunt each summer."

I paused to consider the commitment that living arrangement represented.

Up a winding set of stone steps, we came to a door that led to Levade's small but well-appointed apartment. "This is where my aunt used to stay." Levade pushed the heavy door open, and it squeaked on its hinges. The room was orderly and efficient, attributes I'd come to associate with Levade and her horse training, at least the training of Alizar. Suddenly something blew through the air, slamming into the furniture, and Sass let out a large howling growl.

"Now that's the kind of greeting I expect," I said, then smothered Levade in more kisses, unable to separate what I wanted to say from what I felt. This woman was younger than I, more refined in many ways, psychic, and mentally very strong. How could this work for more than the time it took to make us horribly sad and angry when we broke up? *But I have a lot to offer too. I'm talented and funny, and let's not forget addictive.*

"I hear your mind clicking away. You're already worrying about what might happen, or might not happen, down the road between us. And yet, those worries never bothered you with men."

"Because I didn't care."

"And now you do. And that's love. And there's risk. And you need to stop thinking so much."

"That's what writers do. We think about happy endings and will they turn out that way, and what would happen if they didn't."

"Let me see if I can disengage your brain." Levade slipped out of her clothes and then yanked my shirt off me and unzipped my pants, pushing me onto the bed and kissing me with such fervor that it created visible signs of melting. Then she pulled back and looked into my eyes. "I'm in love with you," she said quietly.

This time my response was immediate. "I'm so incredibly in love with you. You're my soul mate, the one person who completes me. I'm not happy unless I'm with you."

She cocked her head to one side, gave me her beautiful smile, and said cheerfully, breaking the romantic mood, "Good!"

I laughed at her response, as if she were the instructor, pleased that I'd finally understood the lesson and had gotten the answer right. Then her look changed to longing, and she slid her naked body farther up on my chest and guided my face into the deepest part of her, as I clenched her buttocks tightly in my hands and thrust her into me, and she moved rhythmically, pounding and pounding, and climaxing too soon.

I was insane for her, and I rolled her over onto her chest, stretched myself onto the length of her back, and reached underneath her, seeking out the most sensitive part of her, stroking her as she writhed, begging me to give her time to recover, but I would not. I kissed the back of her beautiful neck as I held her open, allowing me to enter, and she bucked beneath me, and her hips pushed up into me, and she tried to muffle her screams in the pillows as she climaxed, shaking and shattered.

As I rolled off her and she turned toward me, I could see in her magnificent eyes that she was undone.

"That was beyond phenomenal," she whispered.

I cocked my head to one side, gave her a big grin, and imitated her unromantic, cheery reply, "Good!" I said, and she giggled uncontrollably and punched me playfully, and I loved who she was.

❖

I was snuggled up to Levade, lounging on a huge leather couch with her head leaning back against my chest and my arms wrapped around her. It made me think of the picture of Angelique and Aunt Alice on the cabin porch swing, in this same position. "This is what love looks like," Ramona had said. Basking in the warmth of lovemaking, staring at the snow-covered pasture where white horses in blankets were cavorting, I knew she was right.

"Ramona has pictures of Angelique and Alice together. We should frame them and hang them in here," I said, already mentally moving in, and Levade smiled at me.

The phone rang, and as if conjured up, Ramona's voice was distinctive and irritated at not knowing where I had been.

"I thought you were dead! I even called Sam, and he said you left the coffee pot plugged in, and a gorilla-porn pepper shaker for Marney, and you just evaporated."

Good old Sam, I thought. He can definitely keep a secret.

"For all I knew, you fell in the lake or were attacked by brother-of-Frank!"

"Did Frank have a brother?" I glanced down at Levade, wondering if we would have more siblings to deal with, and Levade rolled her eyes.

"No! Thank God!" Ramona shouted.

"I'm in Illinois at a very expensive horse farm," I said.

"Why, for God's sake?" she exclaimed.

"I'm with Levade."

Ramona's voice warmed up. "Ah, I see. No waiting till spring. You'll be back in New York soon. Wait and see."

"I can't wait," I said, and left her to interpret that remark.

Her voice contained a smile. "Well, write something, will you?"

When I hung up, Levade pulled away from me. "You talk to her a lot. Are you attracted to her?"

"You're psychic. You should know the answer to that," I teased.

"I want to hear it from you." She punched me playfully.

"My publicist? No! Of course not. This jealousy over other women, is that a lesbian thing?" My mind was already zipping ahead to a time when I would have to defend all my actions and learn the intricacies of living with Levade.

"Here's a 'lesbian thing,'" she said, and shoved me onto my back, her hot mouth devouring mine. I pulled back to gaze into those gorgeous blue eyes, and then, wet with wanting, I kissed her again mercilessly, submerging myself in her, lost in the throbbing heat of our desire. My waiting was finally over, and despite how long it had taken me to find Levade, her love was worth waiting for. She was the other half of me, my ethereal blue lake and the point of my existence. The woman I would spend the rest of my life with, if she would have me. And why wouldn't she have me, I thought. I'm addictive.

We made love all night, as if making up for all the years we'd been without each other. At dawn, as horses nickered in their stalls and the sun rose over the snowy fields, I lay with Levade asleep in my arms, and it was then I realized that Angelique had fulfilled her promise to me, made on that first plane ride to the Northwoods: I had found passion I never knew existed.

Thank you, Angelique, and give my love to Aunt Alice.

About the Authors

Andrews & Austin began as theatrical and movie-of-the-week writers in L.A. Andrews was raised on her grandmother's horse ranch in Oklahoma, while Austin spent time on her aunt's cattle ranch in New Mexico. Andrews & Austin now live on their own ranch on the prairie with Icelandic horses, and an assortment of dogs, and cats. They can be contacted at: AndrewsAustin@gmail.com They blog Mondays and Thursdays at www.bossmaresart.com where women's equality converges with equine art. A boss mare is an older, wiser, female horse with the most common sense. Andrews & Austin were recipients of the 2007 GCLS Debut Author Award.

Books Available from Bold Strokes Books

Face the Music by Ali Vali. Sweet music is the last thing that happens when Nashville music producer Mason Liner, and daughter of country royalty Victoria Roddy are thrown together in an effort to save country star Sophie Roddy's career. (978-1-63555-532-5)

Flavor of the Month by Georgia Beers. What happens when baker Charlie and chef Emma realize their differing paths have led them right back to each other? (978-1-63555-616-2)

Mending Fences by Angie Williams. Rancher Bobbie Del Rey and veterinarian Grace Hammond are about to discover if heartbreaks of the past can ever truly be mended. (978-1-63555-708-4)

Silk and Leather: Lesbian Erotica with an Edge edited by Victoria Villasenor. This collection of stories by award winning authors offers fantasies as soft as silk and tough as leather. The only question is: How far will you go to make your deepest desires come true? (978-1-63555-587-5)

The Last Place You Look by Aurora Rey. Dumped by her wife and looking for anything but love, Julia Pierce retreats to her hometown, only to rediscover high school friend Taylor Winslow, who's secretly crushed on her for years. (978-1-63555-574-5)

The Mortician's Daughter by Nan Higgins. A singer on the verge of stardom discovers she must give up her dreams to live a life in service to ghosts. (978-1-63555-594-3)

The Real Thing by Laney Webber. When passion flares between actress Virginia Green and masseuse Allison McDonald, can they be sure it's the real thing? (978-1-63555-478-6)

What the Heart Remembers Most by M. Ullrich. For college sweethearts Jax Levine and Gretchen Mills could an accident be the second chance neither knew they wanted? (978-1-63555-401-4)

White Horse Point by Andrews & Austin. Mystery writer Taylor James finds herself falling for the mysterious woman on White Horse Point who lives alone, protecting a secret she can't share about a murderer who walks among them. (978-1-63555-695-7)

Femme Tales by Anne Shade. Six women find themselves in their own real-life fairy tales when true love finds them in the most unexpected ways. (978-1-63555-657-5)

Jellicle Girl by Stevie Mikayne. One dark summer night, Beth and Jackie go out to the canoe dock. Two years later, Beth is still carrying the weight of what happened to Jackie. (978-1-63555-691-9)

Le Berceau by Julius Eks. If only Ben could tear his heart in two, then he wouldn't have to choose between the love of his life and the most beautiful boy he has ever seen. (978-1-63555-688-9)

My Date with a Wendigo by Genevieve McCluer. Elizabeth Rosseau finds her long lost love and the secret community of fiends she's now a part of. (978-1-63555-679-7)

On the Run by Charlotte Greene. Even when they're cute blondes, it's stupid to pick up hitchhikers, especially when they've just broken out of prison, but doing so is about to change Gwen's life forever. (978-1-63555-682-7)

Perfect Timing by Dena Blake. The choice between love and family has never been so difficult, and Lynn's and Maggie's different visions of the future may end their romance before it's begun. (978-1-63555-466-3)

The Mail Order Bride by R Kent. When a mail order bride is thrust on Austin, he must choose between the bride he never wanted or the dream he lives for. (978-1-63555-678-0)

Through Love's Eyes by C.A. Popovich. When fate reunites Brittany Yardin and Amy Jansons, can they move beyond the pain of their past to find love? (978-1-63555-629-2)

To the Moon and Back by Melissa Brayden. Film actress Carly Daniel thinks that stage work is boring and unexciting, but when she accepts a lead role in a new play, stage manager Lauren Prescott tests both her heart and her ability to share the limelight. (978-1-63555-618-6)

Tokyo Love by Diana Jean. When Kathleen Schmitt is given the opportunity to be on the cutting edge of AI technology, she never thought a failed robotic love companion would bring her closer to her neighbor, Yuriko Velucci, and finding love in unexpected places. (978-1-63555-681-0)

Brooklyn Summer by Maggie Cummings. When opposites attract, can a summer of passion and adventure lead to a lifetime of love? (978-1-63555-578-3)

City Kitty and Country Mouse by Alyssa Linn Palmer. Pulled in two different directions, can a city kitty and country mouse fall in love and make it work? (978-1-63555-553-0)

Elimination by Jackie D. When a dangerous homegrown terrorist seeks refuge with the Russian mafia, the team will be put to the ultimate test. (978-1-63555-570-7)

In the Shadow of Darkness by Nicole Stiling. Angeline Vallencourt is a reluctant vampire who must decide what she wants more—obscurity, revenge, or the woman who makes her feel alive. (978-1-63555-624-7)

On Second Thought by C. Spencer. Madisen is falling hard for Rae. Even single life and co-parenting are beginning to click. At least, that is, until her ex-wife begins to have second thoughts. (978-1-63555-415-1)

Out of Practice by Carsen Taite. When attorney Abby Keane discovers the wedding blogger tormenting her client is the woman she had a passionate, anonymous vacation fling with, sparks and subpoenas fly. Legal Affairs: one law firm, three best friends, three chances to fall in love. (978-1-63555-359-8)

Providence by Leigh Hays. With every click of the shutter, photographer Rebekiah Kearns finds it harder and harder to keep Lindsey Blackwell in focus without getting too close. (978-1-63555-620-9)

Taking a Shot at Love by KC Richardson. When academic and athletic worlds collide, will English professor Celeste Bouchard and basketball coach Lisa Tobias ignore their attraction to achieve their professional goals? (978-1-63555-549-3)

Flight to the Horizon by Julie Tizard. Airline captain Kerri Sullivan and flight attendant Janine Case struggle to survive an emergency water landing and overcome dark secrets to give love a chance to fly. (978-1-63555-331-4)

In Helen's Hands by Nanisi Barrett D'Arnuk. As her mistress, Helen pushes Mickey to her sensual limits, delivering the pleasure only a BDSM lifestyle can provide her. (978-1-63555-639-1)

Jamis Bachman, Ghost Hunter by Jen Jensen. In Sage Creek, Utah, a poltergeist stirs to life and past secrets emerge. (978-1-63555-605-6)

Moon Shadow by Suzie Clarke. Add betrayal, season with survival, then serve revenge smokin' hot with a sharp knife. (978-1-63555-584-4)

Spellbound by Jean Copeland and Jackie D. When the supernatural worlds of good and evil face off, love might be what saves them all. (978-1-63555-564-6)

Temptation by Kris Bryant. Can experienced nanny Cassie Miller deny her growing attraction and keep her relationship with her boss professional? Or will they sidestep propriety and give in to temptation? (978-1-63555-508-0)

The Inheritance by Ali Vali. Family ties bring Tucker Delacroix and Willow Vernon together, but they could also tear them, and any chance they have at love, apart. (978-1-63555-303-1)

Thief of the Heart by MJ Williamz. Kit Hanson makes a living seducing rich women in casinos and relieving them of the expensive jewelry most won't even miss. But her streak ends when she meets beautiful FBI agent Savannah Brown. (978-1-63555-572-1)

Date Night by Raven Sky. Quinn and Riley are celebrating their one-year anniversary. Such an important milestone is bound to result in some extraordinary sexual adventures, but precisely how extraordinary is up to you, dear reader. (978-1-63555-655-1)

Face Off by PJ Trebelhorn. Hockey player Savannah Wells rarely spends more than a night with any one woman, but when photographer Madison Scott buys the house next door, she's forced to rethink what she expects out of life. (978-1-63555-480-9)

Hot Ice by Aurora Rey, Elle Spencer, Erin Zak. Can falling in love melt the hearts of the iciest ice queens? Join Aurora Rey, Elle Spencer, and Erin Zak to find out! (978-1-63555-513-4)

Line of Duty by VK Powell. Dr. Dylan Carlyle's professional and personal life is turned upside down when a tragic event at Fairview Station pits her against ambitious, handsome police officer Finley Masters. (978-1-63555-486-1)

London Undone by Nan Higgins. London Craft reinvents her life after reading a childhood letter to her future self and in doing so finds the love she truly wants. (978-1-63555-562-2)

Lunar Eclipse by Gun Brooke. Moon De Cruz lives alone on an uninhabited planet after being shipwrecked in space. Her life changes forever when Captain Beaux Lestarion's arrival threatens the planet and Moon's freedom. (978-1-63555-460-1)

One Small Step by Michelle Binfield. Iris and Cam discover the meaning of taking chances and following your heart, even if it means getting hurt. (978-1-63555-596-7)

Shadows of a Dream by Nicole Disney. Rainn has the talent to take her rock band all the way, but falling in love is a powerful distraction, and her new girlfriend's meth addiction might just take them both down. (978-1-63555-598-1)

Someone to Love by Jenny Frame. When Davina Trent is given an unexpected family, can she let nanny Wendy Darling teach her to open her heart to the children and to Wendy? (978-1-63555-468-7)

Tinsel by Kris Bryant. Did a sweet kitten show up to help Jessica Raymond and Taylor Mitchell find each other? Or is the holiday spirit to blame for their special connection? (978-1-63555-641-4)

Uncharted by Robyn Nyx. As Rayne Marcellus and Chase Stinsen track the legendary Golden Trinity, they must learn to put their differences aside and depend on one another to survive. (978-1-63555-325-3)

Where We Are by Annie McDonald. Can two women discover a way to walk on the same path together and discover the gift of staying in one spot, in time, in space, and in love? (978-1-63555-581-3)

A Moment in Time by Lisa Moreau. A longstanding family feud separates two women who unexpectedly fall in love at an antique clock shop in a small Louisiana town. (978-1-63555-419-9)